NANNY WITH BENEFITS

A TEMPERANCE FALLS ROMANCE

LONDON HALE

NANNY
with benefits

LONDON
HALE

Edited by Lisa Hollett of Silently Correcting Your Grammar, LLC

Cover Art © Brighton Walsh

Digital ISBN: 978-1-944336-27-1

Paperback ISBN: 978-1-944336-28-8

For inquiries, contact London Hale at london@londonhale.com

LONDON HALE

To wine,
because if you think we write sober, you're mistaken.

chapter one

IT'D BEEN A year and a half since Bailey had shown up on our doorstep, hoping to become Max's live-in nanny, and I still wasn't used to her. I hadn't quite figured out how to get rid of that punch to my stomach whenever I looked at her. That jolt to my chest when she'd turn her gaze my way and smile. That tightness to my cock whenever that husky laugh of hers left her lips.

Since it was obvious it wasn't anything that was going away, I'd functioned by ignoring it. Or I'd attempted to anyway. It wasn't exactly easy to do when the subject of your infatuation lived in your house, occupying the bedroom next to your own.

Even worse than the pull I felt toward her was how easy it was for me to pretend this whole thing was real. That I wasn't looking at Bailey, my nanny, waving from across the street while holding my son's hand. But that I was looking at my family. It wasn't hard to picture—Max shared her coloring, his fair skin matching hers and his dark brown hair only a shade or two lighter than hers. Besides that, though, it was obvious how much she loved him. On the handful of times we'd taken trips to the mainland, she'd gotten mistaken for his mom more than once.

That was something that never happened in Temperance Falls, of course. Everyone knew of the tragic car accident that had taken Max's mom—my wife—away. We'd been the talk of the island in the time since then. As much as I loved this place, loved it for Max, sometimes I wished we had the anonymity of a larger city. Where no one knew our business. Where I didn't get asked at the grocery store almost two years later how everything was going at home, if I was handling things okay. Trouble was, everyone on the island still saw me as one-half of a whole that would never be again.

But I'd moved on. I'd loved my wife more than anything, had thought I'd spend the rest of my life with her while raising a family. But it had been almost two years since she'd died. I'd mourned her death, and I'd mourned the loss of the life I'd pictured us having together. I'd had to, because I had Max to think about. I couldn't spend my days wishing for something that would never be when I had a sad three-year-old who didn't understand why his mom wasn't coming back. I'd had to make things normal for him again, and I'd done that by grieving and moving on. It was a healthy step in the right direction, yet with every question from a well-meaning neighbor or friend or relative, it made me feel like I'd done something wrong in getting on with my life.

Or attempting to.

I'd come to the point where I'd contemplated dating again. Trouble was, it seemed the only person I had the capacity to feel any sort of attraction to was my too-young nanny. Wasn't that just a kick to the nuts?

I crossed Main Street after saying goodbye to my cousin Brandon, attempting to discard the words he'd said to me. How he'd said Max and Bailey were my *beautiful family*. The gossip train had been going a mile a minute since Brandon and Genesis, his daughter's best friend, had gotten together. It was all I'd heard for the past week in the hospital cafeteria. I knew what that was like—had been living it for far too long—but his situation was something completely different. He'd changed his whole life for a girl. Attraction or not, that wasn't something I was willing to do again.

Bailey stood with a tight grip on Max's hand as he bounced at her heels, waiting for me to get across the street, dancing like he had ants in his pants. I knew he wanted to drop her hand and run to me, but after a scary near-miss with a car speeding through a crosswalk when we'd visited Chicago one weekend, the rule was no letting go of hands without permission. Even while we were on the island where the speed limit topped twenty-five in most places, we didn't take chances.

"Daddy!" Max looked up at Bailey, silently asking

for permission to let go of her hand once I was close enough. She gave him a quick nod and released her hold, which was all the notice I had before thirty-five pounds of excitable five-year-old jumped into my arms.

"Hey, buddy. How was the park?"

"*So* fun. Bee went down the slide with me!"

"Bailey *tried* to go down the slide with you." She rolled her eyes as she fell into step next to me. With a wry smile directed my way, she said, "Bailey got stuck."

I couldn't help the laugh that broke free, picturing her getting stuck on the twisty slide. "How'd you get down?"

"With a bucket of mortification dumped over me and a whole heck of a lot of wiggling." She reached over and tugged on one of Max's legs. "But it made Max laugh, and that's all that matters."

Like always, I was so grateful we'd found Bailey. The search for a nanny had been a long and arduous one, and then Bailey had shown up, and it had been like they'd both fallen in love with each other right then and there. Max had clicked with her instantly, and I'd known immediately she'd be the one. And the connection the two shared hadn't waned at all—if anything, it had only grown.

Max pushed away from my chest, wanting to be let down, so I obliged, setting him carefully between Bailey and me. Without hesitation, he grabbed both of our hands and began swinging them back and forth. Having done this a hundred times before,

Bailey and I knew the score and lifted him off the ground by silent agreement, swinging him into the air as we walked.

After a few swings in the air, he rushed ahead of us, tugging us along behind him. "Daddy and Bee, we gotta hurry 'cause Nana's comin' to get me!"

"Do you even know the way home?" I shook his hand, getting his attention. "I think you might be taking us in the wrong direction," I teased.

"Nuh-uh, Daddy." He lifted his chin in the direction of the too-colorful monstrosity on the corner. "We turn at the playhouse."

"The playhouse, huh? That's a nice name for it."

"I figured Victorian nightmare might not be appropriate," Bailey whispered to me.

I looked down at her, and that was a mistake. Her coffee-colored eyes were sparkling as she stared up at me, the wind blowing strands of her dark hair across her face. One piece got stuck on her bottom lip, which only managed to draw my gaze. Her lips were always a distraction—pink and luscious and full, brushed in some kind of shiny gloss. I wanted to lick it off and see what it tasted like. See what *she* tasted like under it.

Clearing my throat and hoping to God my jeans hid my erection, I turned away from her. "Good call," I said, my voice scratchy and rough. Christ, I sounded like I'd just fucked my way through half the island.

Thankfully, Bailey didn't seem to notice as she chatted with Max, asking him what he planned to do with his grandparents this week during their special time. I should've been paying attention to what he was saying, but all I could think about were those lips. What they'd feel like under mine, what they'd taste like against my tongue, what they'd look like wrapped around my cock.

As soon as we walked in the front door of our house, Max was off, Bailey following behind as she called out orders for him to grab his suitcase and not to forget Bear, his stuffed puppy. What I wanted— *needed*—to do was either jack off or go for a grueling run to work out my frustration. Sadly, neither was an option right then, so I recalled the last surgical procedure I'd performed, going through each step in my mind, until my hard-as-steel cock was at half-mast. Honestly, that was as good as it was going to get when I could smell Bailey everywhere I turned.

A knock came at the door, followed by the sound of my mother's voice. "Josh? Max? Anybody home?"

I didn't have time to answer before Max's booming greeting came down the stairs. Knowing I had about two minutes to say my goodbyes before he dragged my mom out the door, I hurried to the entryway, finding the three of them engaged in conversation.

"And then Bee got stuck on the curler slide!" Max said before he doubled over in laughter.

"Maxwell," my mom said in a stern voice. "That's not nice to laugh at Bailey."

His laughter abruptly cut off, and he looked up at Bailey with worried eyes. "Did I make you sad, Bee?"

She squatted down to his height and rested her hands on his hips. "Never. Now give me a big hug to get me through the week without you. I'm gonna miss my Max cuddles."

With a toothless smile, he wrapped his arms around her neck and squeezed.

Pulling away, she said, "Don't forget about your dad."

I scooped him up and held him close to my chest. "What're the rules?"

"Listen to Nana and Grandpa, no throwing balls in the house, mind my manners," he rattled off with a nod of his head.

"Nice job." I pressed a kiss to his cheek, then set him down. "Be good and have fun. I'll miss you."

Too excited to get to his alone time with his grandparents, he pushed away from me and headed out the door with nothing more than a wave over his shoulder.

"Love you!" I shouted to his retreating form.

My mom laughed and came to give me a hug. "Daddy's old news. He gets the good stuff at Nana's."

"Don't I know it," I said with an eye roll as I returned her embrace. "I'll call tomorrow and check in."

"Sounds good, honey. You two enjoy your time off." She waved before closing the door behind her.

And then it was just Bailey and me, standing in the entryway. Did she feel the sexual tension thick between us, or was it only one-sided?

Running a hand through my hair, I asked, "Have any plans this week? You going home to visit your family or anything?"

"Not this time. My mom's on a cruise with her best friend, so I figured I'd hang out on the island for the week."

I nodded, trying not to think about just the two of us in this house without Max as a buffer. Last year when my parents had taken him, she'd gone back home to visit her family. We'd never had more than an hour or two by ourselves. And I had no fucking idea how this week was going to go.

Still, it wasn't like we should act like strangers. We were adults. There was no reason we couldn't sit down and have dinner together without the conversation of a five-year-old going on around us.

"I'm probably just going to order a pizza for dinner if you want to join me." I shrugged, like it was no big deal. "That is, if you don't already have plans."

She stared at me for a minute, her lips parted in shock before they turned down at the corners. "Oh, well…I sort of have a date tonight."

If I ever wanted to know what it felt like to get knocked out by a heavyweight boxer, apparently I just needed to have Bailey tell me she was going out with another man. Anger and frustration crept over me, red clouding my vision as I thought of her out with someone else, laughing for him, parting her lips for him, kissing him. I clenched my jaw once, twice, attempting to get my jealousy under control. I had no right to feel any kind of claim for her. She wasn't mine, no matter what my fantasies said.

"I see," I finally said. "Is he a friend?"

She shifted on her feet, plucking at the hem of her

sleeveless shirt. "No. Not at all. He's…it's a blind date thing. I don't… He's from the mainland."

I couldn't even focus on how quiet and unsure her voice was—so unlike her usual self. All I heard was *mainland* and *stranger,* and my anger increased tenfold. "You're going to the mainland to meet up with a guy you've never met before?"

She shook her head. "Oh, no. He's coming over here. We're meeting down at Rosie's Place for an early dinner is all."

What kind of schmuck takes a girl like Bailey to a *diner* on a first date? Bailey was the kind of girl you went all out for—the kind you tried to impress, no matter what sort of budget you were working with. I bet he didn't know she would have preferred a picnic in the park to some generic chitchat while sitting across from each other in a ripped booth at the local diner. Fucking amateur.

An amateur she was in no way bringing home to my house.

I knew she was aware of the rules—they'd been in place since she started and had been something I'd decided on before I'd even met Bailey. No bringing dates to the house. When I'd made that rule, it had been because I hadn't wanted Max to feel unsafe in his own home. Now, it seemed, it was serving as the lifeline for my sanity.

Or whatever shred of it I had left.

I cleared my throat, knowing I needed to leave before I acted like any more of an unprofessional dick around her. She was my nanny, nothing more. It didn't concern me if she went out on a date or if the guy she went with took her to a fucking rodeo. She could do whatever she wanted with her life without regard to me.

"Well, I hope you have a good night," I said as I headed upstairs toward my bedroom. I had some frustration to get out, and a run wasn't going to cut it.

"You too, Josh," she called from the entryway, her voice barely reaching me as I walked away from her.

chapter two

BAILEY

DATING SUCKED. Especially when the person you'd been set up on a date with was as boring as the guy who sat across from me. Boring and rude, a winning combination for… Darren…Darien… Damon. Crap, what was his name again?

"I just don't get why anyone would want to live here," No-name said as he shoved a handful of fries in his mouth. "I mean, do you even get cable on the island?"

I fought to hold back my cringe. Didn't he learn any manners growing up? Hell, Max knew not to talk with food in his mouth, and he was five. Please, God, kill me now.

As Darren/Darien/Damon blathered on about all the things those of us who lived in Temperance Falls simply had to be missing out on, my mind wandered.

I missed my little buddy already. Max loved eating at Rosie's Place, and we came here often enough for me to know the owner and all of the waitstaff. Which just made this date even more awkward. I felt as if we were under a microscope, as if people were staring, wondering who this douchenozzle was and why I wasn't here with Max. And Josh.

Oh man—opening the door even an inch to thoughts about Josh, and I was a goner. The diner faded away, the noises disappearing as my mind wrapped itself around images of my boss. He'd looked so good earlier when Max and I had taken him down to Main Street for the afternoon. And when he'd waved from across the street with that bright, wide grin on his face? My libido had kicked up about fifteen notches.

The man was walking, talking masturbation fodder for half the island, and today the whole damn town had gotten to see casual-hot Josh. Scrubs Josh was a fantasy, and dress-up Josh could melt a pair of panties in a snap, but casual-hot Josh? He was my favorite. The man could seriously rock a pair of jeans. It had to be all that running he did. I wasn't exactly out of shape or anything, but Josh put me and my yoga classes to shame. How he found the time to keep in such good shape while being a surgeon and spending as much time as he did with his son, I had no idea. But I appreciated it a lot. The eye candy that was Josh Hutton was spectacular.

"Bailey."

"Yeah?" I looked up to find my date staring at me as if I'd missed something, which apparently, I had.

"Sorry, I was thinking of…ferry schedules. What did you ask?"

"I was wondering if you wanted to head back to your place for a while. Maybe rent a movie or something?"

Oh, hell no. Nope. Not happening. One, I would never invite a virtual stranger back to my place. He could be an ax murderer, and I had the safety of a little boy to think about even though he wasn't there at the moment. Two, Josh might just shit a brick if I came strolling in with some guy.

Josh…he'd seemed a little pissed earlier when I'd said I was going on a date, and I could only assume he didn't want me bringing strange men into his home. I mean, I hadn't really dated since moving to the island because I spent most of my time with Max, but what else could it be? Josh definitely wasn't jealous—the man hadn't even come close to making a move in the eighteen months I'd been in his home. I would have remembered that. Remembered, surrendered, and enjoyed every damn second of it. He might not have crossed the line of professionalism in reality, but I had in my mind many times. Which reminded me, I'd need to make a stop on the way home. Time to lose the non-date.

"My employer doesn't allow me to have guests this late," I lied easily, cocking my head and scrunching my brow in a way I'd picked up from Max. "Besides, the last ferry of the night leaves in twenty minutes. The bridge would take you out of your way by almost an hour."

"Shit, yeah. I forgot about the ferry." He frowned and glanced out the window at the quickly darkening sky. "See? Island living again. I tried to tell my cousin a chick living on Temperance Falls was geographically undesirable, but she was sure we'd get along and it'd be worth it."

I gritted my teeth, holding back how much this date wasn't worth it. "Yeah, I can understand that. How about we just get the bill and head out? Wouldn't want you to miss the ferry."

"Cool. You don't mind going dutch, right?"

———

Ten minutes and the most uncomfortable hug in the history of my life later, I was free. Let Darren/Darien/Damon head back to the mainland—I would rather spend my time on the island I'd grown to love.

As I headed to my favorite store just off the main business strip, I let my mind circle back around to Josh and his attitude earlier. Had I not known him better, I would have sworn he'd been jealous. But that wasn't a possibility, no matter how much I would have liked it. Hot Josh all angry and jealous because I was going out with another guy? Total fantasy material right there. I bet he'd get a little rough with me if that were the case, maybe pick me up and press me against the wall as he demanded I be his and his alone. He'd press that huge cock of his against me and rock his hips until I was a writhing, needy mess. Maybe he'd even be able to make me come. No other partner ever had, but they'd all been boys. Josh was a man and a doctor. I bet he knew stuff. Sex stuff. The kinds of tricks that could make a girl lose her damn mind.

Yeah, that sounded about right.

I nearly jogged the last block to my destination, desperate to get my hands on something new and exciting before heading home. This part of town wasn't exactly a nighttime hot spot save for one place. The garish red lighting in the window set it apart from the dark and shuttered businesses around it, bright enough to reach the church right across the street. Funny, really. A church lit by the lights of the local sex shop.

I yanked the door open and stepped inside, already calmer. Harper, the owner, and her staff never judged me on my quest for the perfect toy. Hell, they kept catalogs and industry mailings for me so I could check out all the latest and greatest toys on the market. Most failed miserably, but every now and again, I managed to get my hands on a winner. I could only hope the latest one I'd ordered was part of the latter.

"Nanny Bailey, you're looking a little flushed already." Harper leaned over the counter, her long hair trailing over her bare shoulders in a way that probably caught the attention of most of the men on the island, her cleavage practically begging to be looked at. If Josh was the favorite masturbation fodder for half the island, Harper was the same for the other half. The woman practically screamed sex with every breath. "What's got you so worked up?"

I shrugged, bouncing on my toes in excitement. "Genesis called earlier and said my new one was in."

Harper laughed, the husky sound nearly sending shivers down my spine. "It did. I've got it right here."

She pulled a box out from behind the counter and handed it over. The cardboard was smooth to the touch, and the box heavier than you'd expect. I ran a finger over the picture on the cover, tracing the curve of the pink vibrator she'd ordered special from Sweden. This was supposed to be the absolute best new model. Long, but not too long, curved to give you that G-spot stimulation. It had little vibrating nubs at the base to keep your clit happy and a rocking motor with fifteen settings for the ultimate in personal pleasure. In a word, it was…

"Pretty."

Harper chuckled again. "I swear, Bailey. You look at vibrators the way I look at chocolate."

"I just want one that works in a reasonable amount of time. Is that too much to ask?"

"No, though maybe something of the human variety would flip your switch a little better."

"Yeah, sure." I huffed and grabbed my wallet. "You find me a man willing to perform an hour of foreplay, and I'll test out your theory."

She raised an eyebrow, pinning me with a serious look. "Honey, if they aren't willing to work to give you yours, they don't deserve to get theirs."

"Exactly. Hence, the need for a good toy."

As Harper rang up my sale—and holy hell would I need to get a second job soon if I kept spending so much on chasing my own orgasm—I flipped the box to read the back. Medical-grade silicone, stronger motor than battery-operated models, and discreet charging station that I could tuck back on the top shelf in my closet so little boys didn't stumble upon it and ask questions. It looked perfect…but looks could be deceiving.

This was the eighteenth time I'd thought I'd found perfection in a sex toy. Only two had even come close. Still, playing with toys, even ones that didn't get me off, had been far better experiences than actual sex. I wasn't kidding Harper when I'd said I needed a man who'd give me an hour of foreplay— my vagina was a hard one to win over, and my clit tended to be awfully particular. I'd never even come close to orgasm from actual penetration, and most guys didn't have the patience to help me out for as long as it took.

They weren't all assholes—I mean, some would even use a toy on me to try to help—they just never understood how hard it was for me to climax. They'd get frustrated, and I'd get to the point where I just didn't want to deal with it anymore, which was why not dating for over a year wasn't a big deal in my mind. I'd been tired of disappointing sexual encounters by the time I was nineteen. At twenty-two, my personal mantra was thank God for silicone.

"This one's a lot more than your past purchases,"

Harper said, frowning as she took the credit card from me.

"I know, but if it works, it'll be worth every penny." I could only hope. Being a nanny wasn't exactly the sort of job where you got rich.

"How about we make a deal?" she said. "You try it out and give me a full rundown—I'm talking play-by-play details so I know how to sell the thing—and I'll give you an employee discount."

I did love a sale. "Would anyone know it was me recommending it?"

"No. I'd keep your name out of it."

"Then sure, why not?"

"Great." She pressed a button on the register, and the total dropped by close to a third. "I can't tell you how many other ladies on the island have similar problems to yours."

"Really?"

"Yes, really. Though some of it is needing an attentive partner, I have to admit. Still, unable to reach climax? That's just unhealthy. Everyone needs a release now and again."

"Don't I know it." My mind immediately shot back to Josh. How did he find his release? He hadn't dated in all the time I'd lived in his house, at least not that I knew of. Maybe he was getting it on at the hospital or something, a thought that made my stomach hurt. Truth be told, if he brought home another woman, I'd be heartbroken. Not that I had any right to be, but still. That would hurt. It was one thing to think maybe someday, and another to know there wasn't a chance.

"All set." Harper handed me back my card and pulled a bag from under the counter. The bell over the door rang just as I was tucking my card back into my wallet. I didn't think much of it or the box in my other hand. The box with the large, hot pink vibrator on the cover. The box I held almost at shoulder height as I delved into my purse with my other hand. Nope, didn't think about it at all.

Until I looked up to find Josh standing five feet away from me, staring at the box in my hand as if he'd just seen a ghost.

chapter three

JOSHUA

TURNED OUT MY right hand wasn't going to cut it. Not when Bailey was out with some twenty-two-year-old dipshit who probably didn't even know how to find a clit. Being surrounded by a house that emitted her scent everywhere I turned wasn't working—not tonight. I needed a distraction, and I knew exactly where to find one.

Living the life of a single dad meant I didn't get to Sin, the local adult toy store, very often—or ever. I'd driven by, of course. Had even walked past a time or two, but I'd never ventured inside. The heavily tinted windows afforded the patrons privacy—or as much privacy as one could expect while visiting a sex shop in Temperance Falls.

But, really, no one would have to know I went. It probably wasn't even busy. I could go in, grab a college coed movie, and be on my way. If the woman in the video resembled a certain raven-haired nanny being fucked within an inch of her life by a sexually frustrated doctor? Well, all the better.

As I stepped inside, the bell on the door announcing my arrival, I was surprised at how welcoming the space was. While it wasn't brightly lit, it also wasn't dark and seedy. The lighting was random but deliberate, creating a mood in and of itself. I was so busy cataloging everything around me at a single glance—the racks of upscale lingerie, the well-maintained display cases of varying toys—I didn't notice anyone else right away.

Until I heard her voice.

My head snapped in the direction of the cash register, where Harper Davis, the owner of Sin, stood behind the counter ringing someone up. And, fuck me running, but that someone was Bailey. I'd recognize that ass anywhere. There she was—my hot as fuck nanny who'd invaded my every wet dream—standing in the middle of Sin. She held a box in her hand—the vibrant picture on the front proclaiming the contents to be a giant pink cock—raised in the air like she didn't care who saw what kind of naughty things she got up to in the bedroom.

Jesus. She was the last person I'd expected to see here, and yet now that I had? I couldn't stop the questions from coming fast and furious. Did she come here often? Was this her first toy? Or was she well-versed in this area? Did she have more at home? Had she used them while I was right next door, seeking release with only my hand?

A dozen images flipped through my mind at that thought. Bailey on her bed, legs spread, pink cock in hand as she teased her clit. Bailey on her knees, face pressed against a pillow and ass up in the air as she slowly fucked herself with the toy. Bailey—

Was looking right at me.

Wide, embarrassed eyes met mine before darting over to the box she still held in the air. "Josh." Her voice was soft and breathless. "I...we...this isn't what it looks li—"

"Welcome to Sin," Harper called to me as she plucked the box from Bailey's hand and dropped it into a bag. "Let me know if you need any help or have any questions."

I flicked my eyes behind Bailey to give Harper a brief nod, but all I could focus on was Bailey's words. This wasn't what it looked like? It looked like she was in a sex shop on her first date. And if that wasn't what it was, that was completely fucking fine with me.

"Either your date is going extremely well, or extremely shitty." With a quick glance, I surveyed the rest of the shop, noticing another woman in the back corner, but otherwise, the store was clear. *Please* let her be here by herself.

"Went. Past tense." She sighed and shifted on her feet, smoothing her hair away from her face. "As in, my date has left the island."

I tried not to let my relief show in my body language, but there was no denying the way the knot in my stomach released—nor was there any hiding the way everything below my belt tightened. No date meant Bailey had no intention of using that toy with anyone but herself. And, fuck me, but those images were going to be the only thing I needed to get some release tonight. A movie with a college coed had nothing on Bailey, even if she was only in my mind.

"I'm sorry you didn't have a good time." I tried to put the right amount of sincerity in my voice, though I was anything but sorry.

She let out a soft huff. "Don't be. I never thought I'd be so relieved to be geographically undesirable."

What kind of jackasses was she going out with? Blind idiots, obviously. "Anyone who thinks you're undesirable in any way, shape, or form isn't worth your time, Bailey."

"That's what I keep telling her," Harper said. "Bailey's a catch." She lifted a brow at me. "But something tells me you already know that."

I hoped she didn't expect a response to that, because what could I say? Yeah, I did know that. I also knew I was a shit for knowing it. That it was inappropriate as fuck, lusting after not only my nanny, but my *seventeen years my junior* nanny.

"Here you go, hon," she said to Bailey, handing over the bag containing my spank bank material for the next three years.

"Thanks, Harper."

Harper's voice softened, but not so much that I couldn't hear it from where I stood. "Hey, what you said earlier? About patience? I think what you need might be right under your nose, if you'd just take the leap."

Bailey glanced back over her shoulder at me, then turned back to Harper. "I'm not that lucky."

"Oh, I think you just might be. Trust me." Harper walked around the counter and hooked an arm around Bailey's, guiding her closer to me. "I know you haven't had a chance to look around," she said to me, "but since you two seem to know each other, I hope you don't mind my asking. Bailey walked tonight, and I have a thing about letting my friends leave from here once it's dark. Be a doll and give her a ride?"

I had to be fabricating the lilt in her voice, right? Because that sure as hell sounded a lot like a double entendre to me, especially when combined with the sassy smirk she shot my way.

Without waiting for an answer from either of us, Harper pressed hands to our backs and guided us toward the door. Honestly, the last thing I needed right now was Bailey in the enclosed space of my car, but there was no fucking way I was letting her walk home by herself. That asshole she'd been out with hadn't even made sure she got home safely? He was lucky he was on the fucking ferry or we'd be having words.

With a nod in Harper's direction, I directed Bailey out the door with a hand at the small of her back, trying like hell to ignore the sexy little gasp she gave at the touch. My Land Rover was right out front, and I stepped ahead of her to open the door for her. As I walked around the back to my side, I tried to talk my dick down, but it was no use. I was in a permanent state of granite cock around Bailey.

It was only a five-minute car ride home, but it might as well have been an hour. I white-knuckled the steering wheel the entire drive, the tension in the car nearly enough to choke on.

"So…" I said into the uncomfortable silence of the car. "We don't have to mention—"

"I just need you to know that I've never taken Max anywhere near that place, and I don't…*do* anything when I'm on work time. Ever. I keep everything well-hidden so he doesn't—"

I held up a hand to stop her. "I didn't even consider that, Bailey. I never worry about your judgment where Max is concerned."

She blew out a deep breath, her shoulders relaxing with the exhale. "Okay. Good. That was just so very awkward, and I wanted to be sure."

"You don't need to say anything more. Whatever you do on your time is your business." Business my cock was very interested in, but there wasn't anything either of us could do about that. I shifted in my seat, hoping to God the interior was dark enough to conceal the way my cock was trying to bust through my zipper.

"You didn't get to buy anything."

I let out a pained laugh. "Oh, believe me, it was a productive trip even if I didn't buy anything."

She cocked her head to the side as she stared at me. "And how's that?"

"I—" I shook my head, my fingers tightening even further on the steering wheel. "I don't think it'd be appropriate for me to say, Bailey."

"You just watched me buy a fluorescent pink, dick-shaped vibrator, Josh. Pretty sure we left appropriate a few blocks back."

"It was awkward, not inappropriate. Those are very different. Believe me."

"I guess, though no matter the word, it was pretty awful." She turned her head away from me, glancing out the window as the neighborhood flew by. "It's not every day your boss finds out you have to get your orgasms from a battery-operated boyfriend."

Oh Jesus, why was she still talking about this? I was going to come in my goddamn jeans like a fourteen-year-old. "Yeah, well, I get mine in hurried shower sessions with my right hand, so I think we're even."

"If you can get off in the shower without running through all the hot water, then we're not even. Not even close."

"You…" My throat was tight, my mouth parched. And I knew I shouldn't ask this question. Should. Not. And yet… "You have a hard time climaxing?"

She let her hair fall, creating a curtain between us. "Hard time doesn't come close to explaining it all."

"I'm sure it's frustrating, but you just need to find someone who's patient. Who'll take his time with you. Get to know what you like…what you need…" *Why* was I telling her that? I didn't want her to find some asshole to get her off, and I certainly didn't want to give her pointers on what to look for.

She snorted, pushing her hair back over her shoulder as she finally looked at me once again. With a wry smile, she said, "Well, if you know anyone like that, send them to my room, okay?"

————

Ninety-seven minutes had gone by since Bailey had said that handful of words to me. Ninety-seven minutes I'd spent talking myself out of being that *someone* who showed up outside her room. Ninety-seven minutes where I'd wondered what would happen if I did.

Somehow, even with those thoughts running through my head of what might happen if I knocked on her door, I managed to reinforce what an epically bad idea it'd be if I acted on anything.

Or I *had*, anyway. Before I'd headed upstairs with the intention of going to bed to work out some of the frustration she'd built up inside me—alone. Before I'd had to pass Bailey's room along the way. Her door was always latched when she went to bed for the evening. But tonight? Tonight, when my control was already tenuous? It was open just slightly, but it was enough so I could hear her. And that was where I stood, directly in front of her barely cracked door, listening to her soft, breathy, sexy-as-hell…*frustrated* moans.

I listened for longer than I should have, hating myself every second, knowing what an invasion of privacy it was to be there. But I still couldn't force myself to move. I was glued to my spot, soaking up every needy moan, every whimper that came from inside.

It was so unlike her to leave her door open that I couldn't help but take it as a sign. Maybe she'd done so on purpose. Maybe she was trying to send me a signal.

Maybe she was hoping I'd be that someone to come to her door.

When another agonized sound reached me in the hallway, I couldn't take it. Not when I thought about her in there alone, struggling to come. Not when I knew I could help her.

Tentatively, I pushed open her door the barest bit, calling out her name as I did so. If she hadn't meant to leave the door open, I wanted to give her the chance to tell me to get the fuck out.

But as the door swung open inch by inch, she didn't give me any warning. And as I listened to her noises grow more and more frustrated, I couldn't stop my feet from moving forward even if I wanted to.

As soon as the room came into full view, I nearly dropped to my knees right then and there. Bailey lay in the middle of her bed, a tank top covering the upper half of her body, but the lower half? Sweet Jesus, from the waist down, she was naked. Her legs were bent at the knees and pressed together slightly, the soft light of a side lamp illuminating enough for me to see peeks of that pink toy as she tried to get off.

"*Fuck*." My expletive wasn't very loud, but it was loud enough to get her attention, her eyes snapping up to mine. She froze, was absolutely still for the longest three seconds of my life, and I was just about to mumble an apology and turn around, mortified that I'd overstepped and obviously taken what was an accident on her part as a sign on mine.

But then she dropped her knees wide, baring herself to me completely as she tentatively reached a hand out to me, and there was no way I was going anywhere.

I took a step toward her, cataloging every inch of her. She was the sexiest fucking thing I'd ever seen, her hair spread out on her pillow, her cheeks flushed— from arousal or frustration, or maybe a bit of both.

"How long have you been at this?" I asked, my voice sounding like I'd swallowed a handful of gravel.

"I don't know." She licked her lips. "Long enough that I'm practically numb."

She'd been trying to get off by herself for so long her clit was numb, and I'd been drinking away my frustration downstairs when I could've been up here, tongue deep.

"Turn it off, Bailey."

She paused for barely a moment before shutting it off. A small bite to her lip later and she tossed the fluorescent toy to the side. "Now what?"

"Now you just lie there and let me get to work."

She stiffened, her knees fluttering inward. "I'm not work, Josh. I don't need you to treat me like one of your patients."

I snorted. I couldn't help it. "This *definitely* isn't how I treat my patients. And if getting you off is the reward for my *work*, I'll gladly do it all goddamn night for you."

With a huff, she rolled her eyes and tugged at the pale blue blanket crumpled under her. "Yeah, well, we'll see if you still say that when my body refuses to give. I don't exactly have a quick trigger."

"You let me worry about what your body's gonna give me. You just worry about how everything feels, okay?" I closed the remaining distance between us, climbing onto the foot of her bed. Grasping her ankle in my hand, I lifted her leg, plucking off the sock she still wore. Then with maximum effort on my part, I took my time and inched my way up her leg, pressing openmouthed kisses along the entire length. I paid special attention to her ankle, the back of her knee, the inside of her thigh, flicking my tongue and making her gasp and moan and reach for me.

And then I repeated the entire track on her other leg, leaving her a panting mess beneath me.

"Do you have any idea how adorably sexy you are, lying here with your pussy on display for me, but still wearing socks and a tank top? Makes me wanna try harder to get to all the other parts."

"You don't have to try at all." She arched her back, lifting her hips like she needed me closer.

Not yet.

"I think we've established that you've had enough guys not trying." I pressed a kiss to her hip, licking a path nearly down to her pussy before moving back up, nudging her tank top up with my nose. "You gonna let me see what you have under here?"

"Be my guest."

Each sexy inch of creamy skin became visible as I pushed the tank top up her chest, pausing once the lower swells of her breasts peeked out underneath. I wanted to tug the top up another two inches, wanted to find out if she had cotton-candy- or mocha-tipped tits. I wanted to know the size and shape—how they fit in my hands. How they felt in my mouth.

But Bailey was in this position because the boys she'd been with hadn't taken their time with her. They hadn't showed her the erogenous zones on her body—hadn't exploited every single one of them.

And I fucking loved that I'd be the one to do it.

With lingering kisses against her stomach, I got drunk on the taste of her. I traced a path from her belly button all the way up, then flicked my tongue against the underside of her breast, my cock nearly bursting in my jeans from the choked gasp she let out.

"Holy shit, that feels amazing."

"See how good it can be when someone takes his time?" I asked as I stretched on top of her, once again ignoring her breasts, as much as it pained me. I wanted her panting for it, wanted her so close to coming, just the suction of my mouth on her nipple would send her flying even further toward release. I sank between her parted legs, pressing against her with a swivel of my hips as I dragged my bottom lip up the column of her neck. "I want you so wet you soak my jeans."

She bucked up against me, grinding her pussy all over me. "Pretty sure that won't be a problem."

I couldn't wait another minute to taste her lips. Pulling the bottom one between my own, I sucked gently, then swiped my tongue into her mouth. Without hesitation, she returned my efforts, her arms going around my shoulders as she gave me everything she had. She worked her little pussy up against me, her legs wrapped around my jean-clad hips. I wanted nothing more than to shed these fucking cockblockers and sink deep, but this definitely wasn't about me tonight. Even if Bailey was writhing under me, primed to fuck.

Needing a break before I embarrassed myself, I pulled back, sliding a hand under her tank top and cupping a breast. Her nipple was hard and sensitive as hell if the loud moan she gave out as my thumb slipped over it was any indication. Unable to hold back anymore, I lifted the tank up and over her head, then descended and devoured her.

Bailey arched and bucked, hands grappling with any part of me she could touch as I lavished her tits with attention. "Fuck," she breathed. "Maybe a little…"

When she didn't continue, I glanced up at her "Harder?" I asked, then sucked her nipple deep into my mouth, hollowing my cheeks. I released her with a pop. "Or softer?" With gentle strokes, I flicked my tongue around her breast, circling her tip.

"Harder. Please."

"Such a good girl, asking nicely." I kissed and licked and sucked. I scraped my teeth against the hard peaks, bit down lightly to see how she'd react. Bailey was an open book, her reactions telling me everything I needed to know to make her lose her mind. Either the guys she'd been with before were idiots who couldn't take direction or jackasses who didn't think they needed to.

Either way, I was thankful for those pitiful fucks because without them, without her abysmal history, I had no doubt she wouldn't be under me and I wouldn't be wearing jeans soaked with her arousal.

"You know what makes me a good surgeon, Bailey?" I asked as I slid my way down her body. I nipped at the underside of her breast. "Patience." I traced her belly button with my tongue. "Precision." I bit her protruding hip, sinking my teeth in hard enough to make her gasp. "And determination."

With hands braced on the inside of her thighs, I held her wide open with my thumbs, exposing every inch of her pretty pussy that had spent the past twenty minutes working itself over on my covered cock.

I glanced up at her from between her legs—my new favorite place in the world. "Ready to see how good I am at my work?"

Not giving her a chance to answer, I leaned forward and took a long, slow lick up the length of her slit, drowning in the taste of her. She was positively drenched, her arousal coating the inside of her thighs, her clit swollen and flushed pink and hungry for attention.

But I didn't focus my efforts there. Instead, I took my time everywhere else. I sucked and licked and nipped at every square inch of her until she was a mess of incoherency. Her legs were shaking, her body covered in a light sheen of sweat, her fingers grappling at every part of me she could reach.

"Oh God, please. *Please please please, Josh.*"

It was that plea that sent me over, the breathy way she said my name at the end. Taking mercy on her, I enveloped her clit with my lips, sucking lightly before pulling back and tracing fast circles around it. I filled her with my fingers, wishing it were possible to eat her pussy all the while sitting back and watching how she fucked herself on my hand.

And she fucked herself, all right. There was nothing inhibited about Bailey as she sought her release. With her hands buried in my hair, she bucked her hips down on my fingers over and over again, growing faster and more insistent with each second. And then with a strangled moan, she came hard.

"Oh *fuuuuuck*." She arched and twisted, her fingers almost painful in my hair as she held me close to her. "I can't… It's never… I've never…"

I groaned against her, loving how tightly her pussy gripped my fingers, sucking me deeper inside, knowing it'd be even tighter with my cock. As she came down, I slowed my efforts, following her lead as she rotated her hips, lazily filling her with my fingers as I brushed my tongue all over her pussy, careful to avoid direct contact with her clit. When she finally released my hair, her hands falling to her sides as she blew out a breath, I pressed a kiss to her inner thigh and slipped my fingers from inside her. Climbing up her body, I pulled the hem of my shirt up to wipe away Bailey's pleasure.

"I'm going to be tasting everything your body *refused* to give for a week, Bailey."

She chuckled softly, almost hoarse, it seemed. "I

think it was more the skills of my partner than any sort of cooperation from my body." With another sigh, she reached for me, and I obliged, gathering her in my arms as I leaned back against her headboard.

"I think you probably just had experiences with jackasses."

"I'd say you're probably right. At least until tonight." She grinned up at me, then walked her fingers down my abdomen, past the waistband of my jeans, until she got to the outline of my cock. "But I wasn't the only one complaining about my lack of orgasms."

Palming my length through denim that was still wet from her, she hummed, then started the torture. Her hand felt so amazing, even through the material, I was ready to combust. After spending almost an hour worshiping her body, combined with the fact that I'd been nearly celibate the past two years, and I was ready to come right the fuck then. Wanting to stave off my impending orgasm as long as possible— or at least until she got my cock out of my jeans—I glanced around the room, desperate for a distraction.

"I've literally dreamt of this," Bailey whispered, inching down my body. "How thick you'd feel in my hand, what you'd taste like. If you'd be gentle on me if I sucked you, or if you'd fuck my mouth. It's one of my favorite—"

The rest of her words got lost among the rapid beat of my heart pounding in my ears. I'd searched for a distraction, and I'd found one. A picture of her and Max sat on her nightstand. It was one of my favorites—Max bent over backward on Bailey's arm, his face pure elation as she smiled down at him, tickling his stomach. That picture—seeing the unrestrained joy on my son's face…joy that had been missing for months after his mother passed away… was as effective as a bucket of ice water over my libido.

I'd managed to piece together my son after devastation, and I'd somehow forgotten that fact in the face of getting lucky. What the fuck had I been thinking?

I stilled her hand before she could unbutton my jeans, swallowing hard at what I needed to do. "I should go." My voice sounded gruff, all wrong. Like I had to force the words out through unused vocal chords.

Her body went stiff, her hand curling into a fist against me. "Wait…what? I thought… Well, I mean…why?"

Removing my arm from around her, I slipped out of her bed and took a step back. "I shouldn't be in here, Bailey. I shouldn't have—" I cut myself off because, really, what was I going to say? I shouldn't have licked your pussy and had you come all over my tongue? I shouldn't have fucked you with my fingers, but at least I didn't stick my cock in you? A+ for professionalism, Doc.

Jesus.

I'd worked so hard to give Max a safe, stable home life after the only world he'd known had been turned upside down, and I just jeopardized it all for an hour in Bailey's bed.

"Josh, wait." She rose to her knees, covering

herself with her sheet as she crawled toward me. "Talk to me. What just happened?"

I shook my head and left her room without a word, closing the door behind me with a soft snick and hoping my lust for Bailey hadn't just fucked up everything I'd worked toward for my son.

chapter four

BAILEY

I WOKE UP the next morning with my eyes crusty from crying, my heart broken, and my pussy still tingling. I would have liked to be able to say that the night before didn't happen, but there was no way to deny it. My boss, the amazingly sexy Dr. Joshua Hutton, had gone down on me and made me come. A total first for me with a partner.

But that wasn't really the bad part. That wasn't the part of the story that made me cringe and want to hide in my room for…well, until I got fired and had to leave. No, the worst part was that he'd hightailed it out of the room like someone had set his ass on fire. After I'd gotten mine and long before he'd gotten anything. I didn't understand it.

He'd been hard, like really hard, and I'd only just started to make a move on him. The poor man had implied he hadn't been with a woman in years—a blow job was the least I could do for releasing me from my partner-induced-orgasm virginity. I had grand plans of a few strokes with my hand before taking him in my mouth and showing him all I could do to make him feel good. And if he'd decided to fuck me instead of coming in my mouth? Bonus for me.

But he'd shot those plans to hell with his *I should go* and his *I shouldn't be here*. As if I were some sort of sexual charity case—the girl whose body hated her and often refused to climax, and the doctor who could show her how good sex could be. I mean, not forever—just that once—because he'd run away and left her wondering what the hell had happened, naturally.

If he wasn't so kind and sweet, I'd think he was a jackass.

But it was morning again, another day, another chance to see what happened. Josh wasn't the type to be cruel, so something had to have gotten under his skin and made him run like that. I needed to figure out what so we could move past it. Even if we went back to just boss and employee—which would suck in so many not-allowed-to-suck ways.

I groaned and rolled out of bed, heading for the shower, needing a little extra time to psych myself up for what I knew would be an awkward moment downstairs. Hopefully, I'd get Josh to talk to me and we'd figure things out.

————

The second I walked into the kitchen, I knew this was not going to be the morning to figure things out.

Josh sat at the kitchen table, sexy-as-fuck reading glasses perched on his nose as he read on his iPad, his shoulders set and his spine stiff. The man was on the defensive. This was going to suck.

"Good morning," I said, keeping my voice quiet and my steps light as I made my way to the cabinets.

Josh startled, as if he hadn't expected me. A fact that made my stomach tighten even more.

"Morning." He went back to his iPad, ignoring me.

I made a cup of coffee, my throat tight and my stomach twisting the entire time. I'd expected more from him, but apparently, I wasn't going to get it without pushing. One of us needed to be an adult and start the conversation, no matter how awkward it would be. I'd been hoping it would be Josh, that he'd step up and be the one to calmly discuss his actions and where we went from there. Apparently, he had other plans. Plans that included ignoring the elephant trampling through the room. I wasn't willing to do the same, though.

So as I settled in across from him at the table, I took a deep breath and readied myself for some serious adulting. "About last night—"

"I'm sorry. I shouldn't have overstepped my bounds." He ran a hand through his hair, refusing to even look me in the face. "I know it's a lot to ask, but I'm hoping we can just forget it ever happened."

It was a lot to ask. Too much, in fact. "Yeah, that's not happening. The only thing ignoring last night is going to do is make things worse."

His head jerked back, his eyes finally meeting mine. Big, nervous eyes. I hadn't been expecting that from him. Disgust, doubtful but possible. Awkwardness, sure. Distance, definitely. Nervousness? Never. What could he be so worried about?

Ignoring the urge to investigate that look, to interrogate him until he told me what he was so concerned about, I gripped my mug to keep my hands from shaking and went in a different direction.

"Why'd you run out?"

His expression hardened, and he looked away once more. "I think I already made this situation as bad as it could be, don't you think? I went down on my nanny, for fuck's sake. That's not appropriate behavior, certainly not with the woman who's taking care of my son."

I was really getting sick of the word appropriate. "Then why'd you even bother coming into my room?"

He sighed and scrubbed a hand over his face. "Because I'm attracted to you—I always have been. I thought that was fairly obvious. But just because there's attraction doesn't mean it's something I should act on."

I digested those words for a good three seconds, relishing the fact that he was attracted to me. Relieved, even. "So it wasn't a pity orgasm?"

"Jesus, no," he said, frowning as if even the thought was appalling. "Why would you think that?"

"Why wouldn't I? The man I've had a crush on for almost two years finally makes a move, but only after he learns how defective I am. And when I try to return the favor—something I've been dreaming of doing, by the way—he runs." My shoulders sagged, much of the fight draining from my body. "It was so obvious you regretted being with me."

Josh tossed his iPad onto the table, his eyes hard and filled with anger as they met mine. "First of all, you are *not* defective. You came just fine last night."

I blinked. Twice. Josh stared back at me, his lips turning up in a grimace as the seconds ticked by.

"I came *just fine*?" I stressed each syllable, my tone harsh and my words clipped.

He groaned, pressing his fingers to the bridge of his nose under his glasses as if trying to hold back a headache. "Try to forget I said that. I shouldn't be saying things like that to you."

"Why not?"

He laughed, the sound so out of place, I sat back in my chair and simply stared at him.

"Where do I start?" he asked in an incredulous voice. "I'm your employer. I rely on you to take care of my son. Not to mention the fact that I am nearly old enough to be your father."

Sometimes puzzle pieces seemed impossible to put together, and other times they fell into place without issue. I hadn't expected an aha moment with Josh, hadn't planned on actually getting to the root of his problem with me, but his words dropped those pieces in a way that they slid together in my mind and showed me one very clear picture. "Is that it? You want me but think you can't have me because of Max?"

He looked away, avoiding me once more. "I want you, Bailey. I always have. But, I'm sorry. I can't do anything to jeopardize—"

I shoved back from the table, the screeching of the chair drawing him up short. "Do you really think so little of me? Do you think I'd risk that little boy in any way?"

"Bailey, what—"

But I wasn't hearing him. "For fuck's sake, Josh, I'm not stupid or heartless. You weren't the only one who dealt with Max's grief. You aren't the one who wipes his tears away when his doctor daddy is stuck at the hospital for a long surgery, and he gets anxious about losing another person in his life." I stomped across the kitchen, rage fueling every harsh move. "I know how important I am to that little boy, and I'd never do anything to risk that relationship. I thought maybe—just maybe—we could move the attraction between us to the next level, that we could be adults and put Max first while exploring our feelings."

"I'm *trying* to put Max first!"

I slammed my coffee cup on the counter and spun to face him. "No, you're not. You're putting your fears first. Max gets second place."

My eyes burned, tears ready to fall. He really thought I'd leave Max if things didn't work out with us? Did he not know me? Did he not see how much that little boy owned my heart? Max was family, and the fact that Josh chose not to notice that hurt far more than him walking out on me the night before.

I rinsed out the mug and set it in the dishwasher, slamming the door closed. "Just so you know, no matter what happens with us, I'd never walk away from Max. Ever."

My tears began to fall, leaving wet streaks behind on my cheeks. I needed to go, needed to get away so I could settle down before I said something I really regretted. Before he saw how much he'd hurt me and tried to placate me with words he didn't mean.

I wasn't above launching one final hit below the belt, though.

"You keep your fears company," I said as I headed out of the kitchen. "I've got a lunch date to get ready for."

JOSHUA

———

I fucked up. There was no other way to describe it as I watched Bailey storm out of the kitchen, her irritation cloaking the room even after she left. I plucked off my glasses and scrubbed my hands over my face with a groan. How had I let this get so screwed up?

I'd gone to bed last night with the smell of her all over me, so *sure* walking away had been for the best. That instead of thinking with my cock, I was finally thinking with my head and doing the logical, responsible thing. For all of us.

Not only did I have Max to worry about, but I knew Bailey didn't come from a lot of money, and her employment with me was the only reason she was able to stay on the island while taking online classes to complete her business degree. I hadn't wanted to do anything to jeopardize her future. Not that I'd *ever* fire her—Max loved her too much, and the feeling was mutual between them—but if she got uncomfortable, I didn't want to put her in a situation where she had to make the choice between her livelihood and her happiness.

But then, in true Bailey fashion, she'd taken a sledgehammer to my thinking, busting through every preconceived notion I had, and made me see things from her perspective. And from her perspective? I was the Grade A asshole who walked out on her five minutes after she came, not the responsible parent I thought I was being.

She'd been right—I was letting my fear guide my decisions. Even shittier was that I'd even convinced myself it had been for Max when it was clearly to protect myself.

I sat at the kitchen table, staring at the place she'd just escaped through—for a *date*, apparently. The thought of her out with someone else about killed me. It didn't matter if the guy was an immature twenty-two-year-old or a forty-two-year-old business owner, I didn't like it. I *hated* it. Hated the thought of someone else buying her a meal, sitting across from her, and soaking up every one of her smiles. Someone else being on the receiving end of her laughter, hearing about her day. *I* wanted to be that someone—had wanted it for a while.

I'd had a taste of what it could be like to be with Bailey, and now I wanted the whole damn meal. If she was willing to explore this thing between us—if she wasn't worried about the possible outcomes—then I was going to trust her judgment and push away my reservations.

But now, thanks to my asinine assumptions and my asshole reactions, I had a dog house to get out of. The only other time I'd seen Bailey that pissed off had been when a little shit at Max's school had swiped his lunch and pushed him down on the playground, ripping his jeans and cutting open the skin on his knees. She might not have been Max's biological mother, but the mama bear was fierce and alive inside her, that was for damn sure.

My plans would have to wait until tonight, but I knew exactly what to do. It wasn't anything extravagant or outrageous, because that wasn't Bailey. I just hoped it was enough.

I had a couple stores to get to, but first... I grabbed a stack of Post-it notes from the drawer, uncapped a pen, and wrote a few quick notes to her. Leaving them around where I knew she'd see them, I smiled for the first time that morning and went to grab a quick shower before heading out.

I wasn't happy about her going out with some

other dick, but I couldn't exactly stop her. I could, however, do everything in my power to make sure she knew how sorry I was and that she thought of me the whole time.

chapter five

I DIDN'T ACTUALLY have lunch plans, but I figured getting out of the house would be a good idea. I was too angry, too hurt to stick around. If Josh tried to talk to me right then, I'd probably say something I'd regret. Or cry. God, I didn't want to cry in front of him.

Still, it surprised me when I heard Josh's car start and pull out of the driveway. Surprised and hurt, if I was being honest. Guess I really wasn't worth pursuing. I watched out my window as he left, a sense of hopelessness swamping me. That was it. Crush over… Josh had put the kibosh on anything more than an employer/employee relationship between us. I'd have to accept that.

I trudged down the hall, figuring I could walk down to Main Street and drown my sorrows in some ice cream from Scoops, the year-round ice cream parlor. I'd give myself a few days to wallow in the sadness, then I'd need to pull my shit together. Max would be home eventually, and it would be time to go back to work. That little guy needed me, and I refused to let him down.

There was a yellow Post-it stuck to the top of the banister. I hadn't heard Josh come upstairs, though that didn't mean he hadn't. Still, if he was going to fire me, a sticky note was about the most classless way to go about it. My anger flaring back up, I stormed to the note, ripping it off the wood post, ready to tear it into pieces, but the simple words written on it quelled every bit of that emotion.

I'm sorry.

That was it. Two words. The simplest apology known to man and yet so effective. I ran my fingers over the solid black lines. Did he mean it? And what was he sorry for exactly? I was about to take the note back to my room for some serious overthinking when another slip of yellow caught my attention. This one was on the bottom banister, stuck to the wood just like the one at the top of the stairs. I hurried down the steps, anxious to see what the second note had to say. I was not disappointed.

I'm an asshole.

"Yeah, you sure are," I whispered into the empty house. A third note caught my attention, sitting right underneath my keys on the foyer table. This one I walked to slowly, almost afraid of what I'd find. Of what he had to say. The keys jangled as I moved them, the words coming into focus before I'd even plucked the paper from the tabletop.

I wish I were taking you to lunch.

I fought the smile tugging at my lips. The notes were cute, too cute. Almost enough to make me want to drop my guard and wait for him to come home. Almost, but not quite. I grabbed my purse and keys, tucking the notes in my back pocket before heading for the front door. But there was one more surprise for me, one more little square of yellow.

I slept with the shirt you came all over, and now my bed smells like you. I spent all night dreaming about making you come.

I snatched the note off the door, frowning. Words were nice; actions were better. We'd see how things went once the damn panty-melter came home. Meanwhile, I wasn't going to sit around waiting for him. I had my own plans to make, and they entailed a trip to my favorite store.

———

Six hours and one hefty charge to my credit card later, I found myself pacing the length of my room. Alone. Josh had arrived home almost an hour before but hadn't come upstairs. Not that I'd sought him out, either. But he was the one who'd screwed up; he was the one leaving apologetic notes and dirty thoughts for me to find. He needed to make the first move. I just wished he'd make it already.

I was about to say screw it and storm downstairs to see what in the world he thought he was doing when a soft knock sounded. I stared at my closed door, unsure if I should walk over to open it or not. Whatever happened next would change everything. I knew it, could feel the gravity of the situation pulling at me. Would Josh still be apologetic? Or would he have spent his time deciding I wasn't worth the risk after all?

There was only one way to find out.

"Come in," I called, leaning back against my dresser for support.

Josh opened the door, peeking his head around the corner until he saw me. "Hi."

Oh hell. One word, and my poor panties were already soaked. What was it about this man? How did he have such a hold over me? And why did I like it so damn much?

"Hey." My voice sounded off, maybe a little breathy. A tad on the way to phone sex operator. Lovely. "Come on in."

He pushed thc door the rest of the way open and stepped inside. "Did you find my notes?"

I nodded, clutching the edge of the dresser to keep from throwing myself at him. He dreamt about making me come. "I did."

His smile faltered, and for a moment, he looked almost unsure of himself. But then his eyes met mine again, and that killer confidence was back. "How was lunch?"

Josh kept his jaw stiff, saying the words through

clenched teeth. Looking a little frustrated and a lot jealous. And while the young girl living inside of me liked the idea of a man like Josh Hutton jealous over her, the adult in me knew that was a treacherous road to choose. Time to be an adult once more.

"I didn't have a lunch date," I said, pushing off the dresser and stepping closer to him. "I told you that because I was angry and upset, but it wasn't true. I ran a few errands by myself this afternoon."

Everything about him seemed to sigh in relief. It was almost like a wave had washed over him, knocking off the hurt and uncertainty and jealousy. This time, he walked over to me, crossing the room in three easy steps, never dropping my gaze for a second. "I'm sorry."

So sincere. So true. Two words that meant so much to me. He reached up and tucked my hair behind my ear before running his finger over my cheek.

"I know. I read the note." I grabbed his hand and held it against my face. A little softness in exchange for some hard truth. "You're also an asshole, like you said."

His hand froze, his eyebrows sliding up his forehead. And then he laughed. "That I am." Another rub of his fingers along my face, then down my neck to caress my collarbone. I shivered, goose bumps rising across my skin at his simple touch. "I'm still sorry."

"I forgive you," I said softly, meaning every word.

Josh stared down at me, some sort of emotion swirling in his eyes. Passion perhaps, maybe pure old lust. Whatever it was, I wanted to be part of it.

"Do you have plans tonight?" he asked.

"No, I never make plans for Saturday nights." I shrugged, unable not to. "That's family picnic night in the Hutton household."

He smiled, dropping his hand to weave his fingers with mine. "Will you come downstairs with me?"

I nodded and followed him, fighting to keep my breathing normal. I had no idea what he had planned, no idea what was coming, but I was in. Totally, completely, one-hundred-percent in.

"You mentioned having a crush on me for years," Josh said as he led me down the stairs. My face heated, but I couldn't deny it. Especially not when he glanced back at me with that serious expression on his handsome face. "I want you to know I've been paying attention that whole time, too. I tried not to because I didn't think I should, but everything about you calls to me, Bailey. I hope I got it all right."

Before I could ask what he meant, we hit the bottom of the stairs and turned the corner into the living room. Normally, it was a simple room—couch, love seat, chair, two side tables, and a large television in a built-in bookcase thing. On family picnic nights, Max usually had a stack of blankets and stuffed animals, I'd have a pillow or two, and Josh would have a pizza with plates and juice boxes set out for all of us.

Tonight was not a normal night.

There were no cartoons on the big screen. Instead, I recognized the opening credits to one of my all-time favorite movies. The one I always watched alone because I'd quote every line and cry at every cheesy emotional scene. On the floor was definitely a blanket, but instead of a pizza box and stuffed animals, the blanket was covered in takeout containers from my favorite sushi spot. There were even a couple of coconut cupcakes off to the side from the bakery I liked to call my own personal heaven. But the best, my favorite part, was the vase filled with hydrangeas on the end table.

"The Bloom Room hasn't had hydrangeas for weeks."

Josh chuckled, pulling me into his arms to rest my back against his chest as he pressed a kiss to my temple. "I know. That's what took me so long. I had to take a trip to the mainland."

Words were hard to come by as I took in every detail, every bit of time he'd invested. All my favorite things—some I'd never actually told him about. He'd been paying attention, far more than I'd ever thought possible.

"I…how did you do all this?" I turned and looked up at him, almost ready to cry at how sweet this man could be.

"It wasn't hard—I already knew all your favorites. I just had to get them." He grew serious, staring down at me in a way that made me want to drop to my knees right there. "Is it right?"

I didn't even need to look away to answer that one. "It's perfect."

———

"How's school going?"

I stretched back against the couch, licking frosting from my fingertips. Josh had been all responsible and eaten his dinner first. I chose coconut cupcakes over sashimi. Just this once. "Really well, actually. One more semester, and I can call myself a college graduate. I might even drive down to DC to walk with the people who went through the program on campus."

"That's great, Bailey. I'm happy for you." He stabbed a piece of his spicy tuna roll with his chopsticks, focusing awfully hard. "What do you plan to do after graduation?"

"I have this business idea I'd like to look into, something I worked on for a project last year that I think would do well in the right spot." I lolled my head to the side, grinning. "No offense, but I don't want to work for someone else my whole life."

His shoulders sagged, his body almost visibly deflating, then he nodded. "That makes sense. Max would be sad to see you go."

Now that I knew, now that I had an idea of how much he cared, his emotions were clear as day to me. It wasn't just Max who'd miss me.

"You know, I never said I was leaving," I said. Still smiling. "My dream would be to be able to stay on the island. I love it here, and I don't want to try to start new somewhere else."

I want to stay with you. The words sat on the tip

of my tongue, heavy and demanding, but I bit them back. He wasn't ready for that kind of statement. I didn't mind being a girl who made the moves, but I didn't want to get pushy about it. I'd keep making my intentions clear, and when he was ready, he could act on his own.

Josh grinned again, inching closer. "I know Max would be happy if you stuck around. On the island, I mean."

"Yeah, on the island." Or in his house. Or in Josh's bed, though that was still a bit up in the air. At least for the moment. Something that needed correcting, and soon. "Besides, how can I just up and leave when the only man who's ever actually made me come is right here? That's not something a girl forgets, you know."

Josh had just been taking a drink of his beer, which meant he choked a little at my statement. "The only man?" he said once he'd gotten his breath back. "You can't be serious."

I moved the empty containers aside and plucked the beer bottle from his hand before twisting to straddle his lap. "I am one hundred percent serious. The only man who has ever made me come is you, Joshua Hutton."

He tugged me closer, barely giving me time to get the bottle out of the way before he dropped a little bomb of his own on me.

Josh leaned closer, running his nose along the length of my neck. My head fell back, my body arching toward him as he bit softly on my earlobe and whispered, "Would you like me to do it again?"

chapter six

JOSHUA

THE QUESTION HUNG in the air between us for only a moment before Bailey went boneless in my arms and sighed out a breathless, "Yes, please."

She swiveled her hips, the skirt she was wearing rucked up around her waist as she ground her pussy down on my already hard cock. Yeah, hearing her say I was the only guy ever to make her come? Knowing her orgasms belonged to only me? I'd been hard as a fucking rock from the moment the confession had left her lips.

With my fingers wrapped around her nape, I guided her lips to mine, not waiting a second to slip my tongue inside. I groaned into her mouth, loving the unique sweetness of her. How I could be starved for her when I'd tasted her less than twenty-four hours ago, I didn't know. All I knew was I'd never get sick of this—of her tongue meeting mine stroke for stroke, her body pressed to mine, her hands grappling at my shoulders, pressing her tits to my chest so hard, like she was trying to meld our bodies together.

I pulled back, nipping at her bottom lip as she rode my cock through my pants. "You gonna soak my jeans again tonight?" I asked, knowing the only thing concealing her pussy from me was the thin material of her panties.

"God, I hope so."

"Do you know how hard I was, sleeping in a shirt covered in your come?" I pulled her top over her head, leaving her in nothing but a tiny, see-through bra so light blue it was almost white, her nipples nearly peeking out of the tops of the low-dipped cups. I groaned looking at this goddess in my lap, bouncing my attention between her flushed face, her parted lips, and her heaving tits. "By the end of the night, I'm going to fuck you in my bed so I'll smell you on my sheets for days."

"I don't care where. Just make me come." She arched backward over my arm as I slid my other hand up her torso, cupping one of her breasts through the sheer fabric of her bra. I reveled in her moans as I strummed her nipple with my thumb, loving that I could get this reaction from her.

"The guys you were with before are idiots. Your body is easy to play if you pay attention. For instance"—I peeled down the cup of her bra and pinched her nipple hard enough to make her gasp—"I know you like your tits handled a little rough. Isn't that right, baby?"

"Fuck, yes."

"You love it when I hollow my cheeks, sucking you deep. Wonder what you'd do if I bit them…" I leaned forward, blowing against her nipple. "Let's find out."

I circled her nipple with my tongue before sucking roughly. Testing the waters, I grazed my teeth over it. She sighed, running her fingers through my hair as she rocked herself in my lap. Sweet reaction. But I didn't want sweet. I wanted the girl who'd fucked herself on my fingers. I wanted Dirty Bailey. Without preamble, I bit down and tugged, flicking her hardened tip with my tongue.

She gasped and dropped her head back, bucking against me harder as a full-body shiver racked her.

"I haven't even touched your pussy yet, and you're already on the verge of coming. Is it because I listen to your body? Or do you think it's *me*?" I repeated the action on her other breast, making her nearly incoherent—moans and broken words tumbling from her mouth as she dry-humped the shit out of me. "Am I the only one who can get you this worked up?"

"Yes. Only you."

"You know what that means?" I asked as I laid her back on the blanket. Her legs fell open as her skirt pooled around her waist, giving me a glimpse at panties in the same pale blue material that matched her bra. Panties that were completely fucking soaked. I reached out, running a finger along her slit, pressing hard when she moaned louder as I reached the top. "This pussy's mine, isn't it?"

"Only if you treat it right."

My mouth actually watered as I looked down at this sexy as fuck girl spread out beneath me. I needed her taste on my tongue again, needed to swallow her come, knowing I was the only one who could evoke that reaction in her. I gripped the sides of her panties and yanked them off, then didn't even let her legs settle back on the ground before I covered her pussy with my mouth.

She was drenched, and I licked up every drop, eager for more. A stream of nonstop curses left her lips, eventually fading into garbled words, then solid moans as I sucked her clit, sliding one, then two fingers inside her.

I pulled back and looked up at her, pumping my arm to match the movements of her hips, studying how she liked to be fucked. "Open your eyes, Bailey." I waited until she complied, then licked my lips. "You see how wet you made my face? That's proof your pussy loves my tongue."

Dropping down, I flicked her clit with my tongue, again and again and again until every inch of her body was coiled tight, preparing for release. Moving back, I replaced my tongue with my thumb, flicking it against her clit as I curled my fingers inside her and pressed down on her lower stomach with my other hand. "Now give me what's mine."

She reached out, grappling for me, her nails digging into my forearms as she stared at me in wonder, her mouth hanging open as her pussy tightened around my fingers.

"Just a little more…" I leaned down and captured one nipple in my mouth, biting down on it, and then she was flying. Her pussy squeezed my fingers, sucking them in deeper as she came all over me. *Jesus*, I wanted to feel that on my cock. "That's it, baby. That's it."

I circled her clit with my thumb and braced a hand next to her head, leaning down to kiss her. She licked every drop of herself off my lips, her arms tugging me closer. "That was even better than last time. How can I still want more?"

Pulling my fingers from inside her, I reached back and tugged my shirt over my head. "Think you can give me another while my cock's inside you?"

"I—I don't know…" She tensed in my arms, darting her eyes all over like she was nervous. Like she was worried she'd disappoint me if she couldn't come.

"Relax, baby. Even if you don't, we're going to have fun trying, aren't we?" I unbuttoned my jeans just far enough to pull my cock out, then grabbed a condom from my wallet. Couldn't even wait long enough to pull my pants all the way off before I got inside her.

Once I was wrapped up, I ran the head through her slit, watching her face as I did so—always reading her reactions. She melted when I rubbed against her clit, her eyes fluttering closed. When I swept my cock lower, pushing just the head inside before pulling out, she whimpered, working her hips closer to me. My girl was hungry to fuck.

I knelt between her thighs, sitting back on my

heels, and hooked my hands under her thighs, yanking her by the hips into my lap until she was braced on the floor by her shoulders. She gasped, her eyes going wide even as her legs relaxed over my forearms. "Josh?"

"I said we'd have fun." I lined myself up and thrust deep, closing my eyes at the pleasure her body gave me. Our moans mixed together when I was fully sheathed inside her. It didn't matter that she was tight as hell, squeezing my cock like a fucking vise. She was so wet, so welcoming, I slid in like she was made to fit me. I blinked my eyes open and looked down at her, flushed and spread out beneath me. "But I'm also going to work like hell to make this pussy sing."

"Oh fuck." She gripped my forearms, her eyes wide as she divided her attention between my face and where my cock was disappearing inside her.

Just like with everything else, I studied her as I moved inside her. Watched her reactions as I tried different speeds, depths, and angles, learning what she liked, what she loved, and what made her moan loud enough to wake the neighbors. Deep, slow thrusts made her gasp and arch, but it was the quick, shallow thrusts that were going to make her come. Once I found that spot inside her, I exploited it, working my cock against it over and over again as I circled her clit with my thumb.

"Josh—" She cut off on a gasp, her back arching as her eyes fluttered closed.

"I know, baby," I said, watching where she swallowed my cock, her pussy spread wide around me. "I told you we were gonna have fun, didn't I? You having fun while I work your pussy?"

"So much. Almost too much."

"Jesus, you feel good. Can't believe you let me inside this heaven." I sped up my thrusts, making sure to keep them slight, my thumb strumming across her clit. "Anyone who has the privilege of being inside this pussy better work hard to get it off. That's *my* privilege now, isn't it? I'm the one who gets to make you come…"

"I'm—fuck, Josh. I don't… I think I'm—" She tightened around me, her back bowing off the ground as she let out a long, low moan.

"Coming. Fuck yeah, you are." I couldn't decide where to look. Watching her face—the wonder, amazement, and desire as she came apart on my cock—or where I disappeared inside her. The pulsing walls of her pussy squeezed the life out of me as I thrust inside, finally pushing as deep as I could. With my hands grasping her hips, I pulled her down on me, fucking her with abandon as I chased my release.

When Bailey reached toward me, saying, "You made me come so hard," I was gone. Chanting her name, I sank deep and came inside her, resting my forehead between her tits as I bowed over her body.

We lay there for quiet moments, my head resting on her chest as she ran her fingers through my hair. After a few minutes, Bailey scratched the back of my neck. "So that's what the big deal's all about."

I breathed out a laugh against her skin, then lifted my head from her chest to look down at her. She was gorgeous, her dark hair fanning out on the blanket beneath her, her tits heaving upward, like she was unconsciously trying to get them closer to my mouth. Pink cheeks, flushed chest, sweat-slicked skin, she looked totally and thoroughly fucked. By *me*. Being the only one who'd ever brought her pleasure like this? Knowing I was the only one who'd ever felt her come on his cock? Said cock twitched inside her, gearing up for another round.

Her eyes went wide as she looked at me, then down to where I was still seated inside her. "Again? Already?"

I gripped the base of my cock and pulled out, quickly excusing myself to the bathroom to dispose of the condom. When I walked back in, she was still lying in the exact position I'd left her—legs and arms spread, totally and completely uninhibited.

"Baby, I could fuck you all night long, and it wouldn't be enough." I scooped her up and ran with her upstairs, pressing a kiss to her jaw. "Now, let's see how many times I can make you come in my bed."

chapter seven

BAILEY

JOSH HAD SKILLS. Serious, undeniable, intense sexual skills. The man had made me come with his mouth and his cock, both feats I'd thought were impossible. He'd proven me wrong. Hell, the second he woke up after a night of sated, clingy sleep, he started proving me wrong all over again.

"Fuck," I hissed, dropping my head back. I was so close already, so tight and swollen and soaked. The man was a sex machine. "I want to come."

"Then work that pussy down on me. Show me how much you want to squeeze my cock."

He thrust from underneath me, his thighs tight against my ass. I'd been on top before, but not like this. Not with my partner's knees bent behind me. Josh had mentioned something about angles and G-spots, but really, I'd been too stuck on his beautiful mouth forming words like cock and pussy to pay much attention to the rest. All I knew was I was straddling the man with his thighs at my back and his hands all over my spread pussy.

Life was good.

I rocked faster, chasing that release, needing one more. Josh thrust up, watching me. Always watching me. Looking for a sign or signal. His thumbs worked in some sort of circular dance over my clit, his hips rolling under mine. The depth in this position, the angle he kept me at, might have been perfect.

I groaned when he pressed his thumbs together, stroking the length of my clit before running around where we were joined. "Can you do that again?'

"I can do it all fucking night if it'll make you come again. You close, baby?"

I couldn't speak, could only nod as he worked my clit like it was his damn job. Faster, harder, I chased that tightness, that need, that tingle giving way to a clench. The one I'd always struggled for. The one Josh was not only able but willing to chase with me, no matter how long it took.

"So close. So close." I threw my head back and grabbed my breast, pinching the nipple. Needing a little bit more. Craving that tiny bit of pain. "I'm going to come so hard."

"But you need it to sting a little first, huh? You need my teeth on you?" Josh didn't wait for me to answer. He sat up instead, his abs flexing beneath me. Before I could even take a breath, his mouth was on my nipple. Sucking. Pulling. Teasing me. But the teasing didn't last. Josh got serious real quick. He sucked my nipple into his mouth and bit down hard enough to make me jump. And more.

I came with a groan that was probably just over the edge of being too loud, not that I cared. Hell, not that Josh cared. He cursed and fell back to the mattress, rubbing his thumbs over my clit, keeping that orgasm rolling as long as possible. But when I was done, when I unclenched, shivering, and curled my body toward his, domineering Josh took over.

He flipped us both, yanking my legs up until my feet were flat against his chest. His thrusts were harder, so much deeper like this. He'd given me mine, and he was taking his.

"You know what it's like, knowing I'm the only one to ever feel that? That I'm the only one who's ever felt you come from inside?" His hips slammed into mine, his motions hard and rough. Almost out of control. "Makes me wanna mark you, Bailey. Show everyone you're mine."

"Oh God. Why is that thought so fucking hot?"

He moved faster, pounded harder, until the only thing in the world was him. The only sound that of our heavy breaths and slapping skin, the only sensation the ones from the heat of his body and the fullness of his cock inside of me.

"Josh." I gasped and rolled my hips up, that familiar tingle slamming down hard on me. Again? How could that be? I'd never brought myself off more than once no matter how hard I tried. But Josh knew what he was doing, an almost proud smile rising on his face as he kept up his pace.

"Ah, baby, you're gonna go off again, aren't you? This pussy's just been waiting for my cock to fill it, hasn't it?" He slowed and dropped his head, giving my ankle a tiny bite before rolling his hips right against my clit. "Give me it. Come all over me."

This time, I didn't come with a groan or a gasp. I screamed as my fourth orgasm of the night—day?— set my body on fire. So strong, so overwhelmingly powerful, even my toes clenched.

Josh grunted out something that sounded an awful lot like *my pussy* before he pressed deep and held himself still, groaning, his abs clenching as he came. Such a sight. This man—this handsome, sweet, smart man— had been my wet dream for close to two years. Seeing him come, watching as his muscles locked down and his eyes closed, as his mouth twisted in pleasure—my imagination hadn't been nearly good enough.

"You're so fucking sexy when you come." The words came unbidden, a truth whispered in the quiet as we both caught our breaths.

Josh chuckled and ran his hands up my legs, kissing my knees before letting them fall to the mattress. "I'm not the sexy one here, Bailey. Believe me."

He grabbed the base of his cock and pulled out of me, excusing himself as he headed to the en suite bathroom. He was back in a flash, kissing his way up over my abdomen.

"We are so not starting again," I said, stretching as his hands skimmed over my waist. He settled on top of me, his hips between my knees, his head against my chest, and his hand stroking and pinching my nipple in an almost unconscious way. Josh was a snuggler. Perfect.

We lay there for quite a while, sometimes whispering to each other, sometimes just enjoying the silence as the sun rose higher outside the windows. It was peaceful and intimate, more so than any other experience in my life. This was what I wanted, what I'd always wanted—a deep, meaningful connection with a good man. True, I hadn't expected that man to be so much older than me, nor had I ever guessed he'd be my boss. But those things fell by the wayside. My heart chose him, my body chose him, I chose him. Nothing else mattered.

Famous last words…or thoughts, in this situation.

"Bee?" The voice that sounded through the house froze us both. Josh's eyes grew wide, surprise evident. "Daddy? Bee? Where are you?"

At the sound of the herd of little feet moving closer, we both jumped up. Clothes-clothes-clothes. I needed my—shit.

"My clothes are downstairs," I hissed, yanking the sheet from his bed and wrapping it around myself.

"Daddy?" Max hollered, sounding tired and whiny. Not a good combination.

"Be right down, buddy." Josh opened a drawer and dug inside before tossing me a shirt. "Put this on."

It was dark cotton, long and soft. And as I went to slide inside the T-shirt, I noticed the lettering.

"Really?" I said even as my smile went wide at the thought of what I was wearing. "Your baseball shirt?"

He shrugged, almost smiling. "I like the idea of

you in my clothes. Especially something with my name on the back."

"You're kind of a caveman, Dr. Hutton."

"Would you believe me if I said I've never been this way before? Apparently, you bring out the caveman in me, baby."

With one final kiss and a heck of a handful of my ass grabbed, he slipped out the door.

"Max. What are you doing home, buddy?"

"Daddy! There you are."

I grinned. God, those two were adorable together. I waited until I heard the sounds of Josh's footsteps on the stairs before heading for the door. Two minutes— that was all I needed to get to my room, throw on some shorts, and head downstairs to see why my little guy was back so soon.

But fate had a way of stepping in and fucking everything up.

Josh's mother walked out of Max's room just as I walked out of Josh's. My eyes met hers, my hands dropping to the hem of the T-shirt with Northwestern emblazoned across the front. There was no doubting what Josh and I had been doing.

"Mrs. Hutton." I nodded, striding for my door as if I hadn't just gotten caught fucking her son. My boss. Oh hell.

"Bailey. I'll give you time to…clean yourself up."

I nodded and hurried into my room, my eyes pricking with embarrassed tears as I shut the door behind me. What had I just done?

chapter eight

THE LIFE OF a single dad wasn't glamorous. It meant shuffling things, rearranging my life in order to make my son my number one priority. Because of that, I didn't even pause as I left a nearly naked Bailey in my bedroom, still smelling of sex, and went to scoop up Max as he trudged up the stairs. His face was devoid of color, his body drained of energy.

My mom stood behind him in the entryway, lugging his suitcase, a frown marring her face. "Sorry to barge in, honey, but I've been trying to call."

I waved her off because, really, even though I'd been halfway to fucking Bailey again, my mom bringing my son home never would have been construed as *barging in*. I'd no doubt feel guilty later about her not being able to get a hold of me when

I knew exactly why I'd been unreachable, but there wasn't time for that now. "What's going on?"

"I don't feel good, Daddy." Max rested his head on my shoulder, and I pressed my cheek to him, immediately feeling how warm his forehead was.

"Fever?" I asked Mom.

She nodded. "He complained this morning of a sore throat and a tummyache, but I figured we'd see how things went. His temp was holding pretty solid at ninety-nine, so we just went about our day. But then he fell asleep watching a movie, and when I checked his temp again after he woke up, it'd spiked to 102. He said he wanted to come home."

"I want Bee," he said, his voice close to tears.

Pressing a kiss to his forehead, I said, "She's right upstairs, buddy. She'll be down any minute, okay?"

He nodded and clung to me, his little fists clutching my shirt.

Turning to my mom, I asked, "Have you been giving him fluids?"

She rolled her eyes. "Honestly, Joshua, I *have* raised children before."

I chuckled and held Max closer to me, rubbing a hand down his back. "I'm not disputing that. But I *am* a doctor. I ask these kinds of questions."

She smiled, reaching out to run her finger down Max's cheek. "I've been pushing water and juice all day, but he hasn't been interested."

"Does your throat still hurt, buddy?"

He nodded against my shoulder, burrowing closer into my chest as I walked us to the kitchen.

"I'm going to get him something now," I called over my shoulder.

"Okay, honey. I'll bring his suitcase up to his room."

Once we got into the kitchen, I set him on the island, then went to get him a bottle of the Pedialyte I always kept stocked in the fridge. You can take the doctor out of the hospital… "All right, buddy. We need you to drink something so you don't get even sicker. You want grape or cherry?"

"*No*, Daddy. I don't want it! It'll make my throat hurt more," he whined, tears pooling in his big, brown eyes.

"How about an ice pop instead?" Whoever at that corporation had come up with freezer pops made of the same stuff in the bottle was a goddamn genius. "Red, orange, blue, or purple?"

"Red, please."

"So polite, even when you feel like doo-doo, huh?"

He gave a watery giggle, his tears subsiding as I gave him the plastic sleeve, watching as he sucked on the ice pop like it was his first meal in a week. I brushed the hair back from his face, trying not to worry at how warm his forehead was against my hand.

When I heard my mom walk into the kitchen, I didn't even glance at her as I asked, "Have you given him any meds today?"

"What? Oh, um, last dose was about four hours ago. He could use another."

I nodded and went to the cabinet above the fridge, grabbing the bottle down and doling out his dosage. "Here, buddy, take this quick, then you can have your ice pop back." Grabbing the plastic sleeve only half full of slush, I swapped it out for the tiny cup of orange liquid.

Max dutifully swallowed it before reaching for his freezer pop once more. His face was pale, his skin clammy. I hoped it was just a virus and he wasn't coming down with strep throat.

"Honey?" Mom asked.

"Yeah," I answered distractedly, never taking my eyes off Max.

"Can I talk to you for a second?"

Something in the tone of her voice had me glancing back at her. Her mouth was set in a thin line, her eyes hard. With a kiss to Max's forehead, I stepped over to where my mom stood by the entryway into the kitchen.

"What's up?"

"Look, honey, you've been an adult for a long time, and I stopped trying to interfere with your life a while ago—"

"Well, that definitely doesn't sound like the intro to you interfering with my life," I said with an eye-roll. "I know you've raised kids before, but Max is mine. If you don't agree with my giving him an ice pop to help keep him hydrated, too bad—"

"No, no. That's not it." She wrung her hands, then brushed a strand of hair away from her face as she straightened her shoulders, seeming to steel herself for whatever she was about to say. "When I was upstairs dropping Max's suitcase off in his room, I saw Bailey."

"Okay…"

"Coming out of your room, half naked."

While I figured this conversation would come sooner rather than later, I wasn't exactly thrilled with it happening right that second while Max wasn't feeling well. "I think it's a little late for the birds and bees talk, Mom."

"Joshua," she snapped. Then in a lower voice, she said, "I don't think I need to remind you that girl has been a blessing to Max these past months."

"No, you don't."

"Then I suppose I also don't need to remind you she's a paid employee and not a prostitute."

I whipped my head around to look at Max, hoping he hadn't heard what his grandmother just said. His focus was intent on sucking the last bit of liquid from the plastic tube. With an exhale, I turned back to my mother. Working hard to keep my temper in check and my voice as low as I could manage, I said, "And I don't think I need to remind you I'm thirty-nine and an adult. I haven't let my mother make my decisions for a long time, and I'm not going to start now."

"I'm not trying—"

I held up a hand to stop her, attempting to push down the anger rushing to the surface. Not able to speak to her right that second for fear of what I'd say, I turned around and got Max down, then patted his butt. "Why don't you head up to your room, buddy. Bailey can help you get into your jammies and get started on a story before nap time, okay?"

He trudged out of the room, his gait slow and lethargic.

Once he disappeared around the corner and up the stairs, I turned back to my mother. "I can't believe you said that while Max was in the room. I can't believe you said that, *period*. That's *Bailey* you're talking about. What the hell, Mom?"

"I shouldn't have done that. I'm sorry. But when I saw—"

I cut her off again because I knew exactly what she saw, and it was still none of her damn business. "Look, Mom, I love you, and I know you're saying this because you're trying to look out for Max and me. But if you *ever* refer to Bailey as a prostitute again, even offhandedly, we're going to have an issue. Max loves her. *I* love her. And that's all you need to concern yourself with."

Afraid I'd say something more I'd later regret, I forced myself to kiss her cheek, then calmly walk away. "Thanks for bringing him home. I'll call you tomorrow and let you know how he's doing."

Without waiting for her to respond, I headed upstairs, still seething from what she'd said. God knew if she weren't my mother, my words wouldn't have been quite so careful or controlled. Needing to see the two people who meant the most to me in the world, I headed straight to Max's room. I stood in the doorway, looking in at him and Bailey snuggled in his bed, him tucked into her side as she read from his favorite book.

My chest actually *ached* at the sight. When my

wife had passed away, I'd never thought I'd feel this again—this overwhelming sense of gratefulness and…love. I never thought I'd *want* this again. I was content going about my life, doing all I could to make up for the fact that Max had only one parent. I never saw myself falling in love again.

But then, I never saw Bailey coming, either.

She swept her way into our lives with her humor and her laughter and her light, and she'd made life better for the both of us. She was the bright spot during very dark days, and she only continued to be that brightness. I had no idea why it'd taken me so long to realize it, why it'd taken me so long to act on it. Regardless, I wasn't going to waste another second thinking about lost time. I also wasn't going to worry about what anyone else thought—my mother included. If I was okay with our arrangement, and so was Bailey, that was all that mattered.

"Bee?" Max asked, tilting his head to look up at her.

Neither of them was aware I'd stepped into the room, a smile on my face as I watched the two of them together.

"Hmm?" she asked, pressing an absentminded kiss to his forehead.

"What's prostitute mean?"

The smile slipped from my face at the same time Bailey's entire body froze.

After a second of silence, she cleared her throat. "That's not a nice word, so we don't use it, okay?"

"If it's not nice, how come Nana said you were one?"

The bottom dropped out from under me, the look on Bailey's face sending a wrecking ball straight through my chest. The color drained from her face, and she worked her mouth to say something, but no words came out. I took a step toward her—to reassure her or take her in my arms or do *something*—and the floor creaked under my foot, alerting her to my presence.

She looked up, meeting my eyes. Where I thought I'd see confusion—maybe hurt or anger or sadness—I saw nothing. Her eyes were blank, her face wiped of all expression. And I absolutely hated that something my mother had said had caused her to shut down.

Knowing I couldn't exactly discuss it freely with Max in the room, but also not wanting to let it slide, I went over to them and sat on the other side of the bed, reaching out to brush his hair back from his face. "Nana shouldn't have said that, buddy. I already talked to her about it." I tried to put as much sincerity in my voice as I could, hoping Bailey would pick up on my unspoken words—that I didn't give a fuck what my mom said. I'd never once thought of Bailey as that—never would, regardless of what we did in the bedroom.

Instead of meeting my pleading look, she closed the book and slid out of Max's bed. Bending down, she pressed a kiss to his head. "I'll be right next door if you need me, okay?"

Then with little more than a gentle hand

smoothing out Max's blankets and one last kiss on his cheek, she left the room, never once looking back at me.

chapter nine

IT WASN'T EVERY day I got called a prostitute. It also wasn't every day that being called a prostitute wasn't the worst thing that happened. I could still hear Max's tired little voice asking me what prostitute meant and dropping the bomb that his grandmother had called me one. And Josh—Mr. Appropriate, Mr. Hundred-Thousand-Dollar Education—comes up with a big old nothing to say back to his son about it.

That hurt far worse than the word and insinuation itself.

Why had his mother called me a prostitute? Well, probably because she'd seen me half naked wearing only Josh's shirt while coming out of his room. I could rationalize her jumping to conclusions seeing as how Josh paid me to live in his house. She wasn't the one who'd sliced my heart right out of my chest.

That honor sat with the good doctor.

Josh could have come up with something to say, some way to defend me to his son, who had no idea what was going on. But no, all I got was a bland "Nana shouldn't have said that." Probably the most accurate thing he'd ever said, and not nearly enough.

I curled around my pillow, fighting to keep the tears from falling. I knew I needed to confront Josh on all the things he didn't say, but I couldn't. Not yet. My heart hurt too much, and my temper was too triggered. If I tried to have an adult conversation right then, I'd end up saying something I regretted. Like I hate you. Or you're an asshole. Or I quit.

God, not that last one.

I couldn't leave my Max. He was the best sort of joy, the pure kind. A little piece of my heart living outside my body even though he wasn't mine. I'd do anything to stay in his life, whether as his nanny or as…more. But if he was going to grow up thinking I was some sort of paid sex partner for his dad? No. That was too heartbreaking even to consider. Which left me in the swirling depths of doubt over what to do.

One comment, and the happiness of the last couple of days was gone.

The clock was glowing bright in my darkened room when a knock sounded on my door. One too loud and forceful to be Max.

"I don't want to talk to you right now." I curled into a tighter ball, wishing he'd go away. Wishing he'd apologize and come in and hold me. Wishing he knew how to make things right, even though I still didn't have a clue what could.

"Bailey, please open the door and talk to me."

I clenched my eyes closed against the pain his voice caused. "I can't tonight. I just…can't."

"Don't shut me out, baby. Please, we need to talk."

We did, but I wasn't ready to. And I was tired of his pushing.

I jumped up, storming to the door, still refusing to open it. "Your mother called me a prostitute, Josh. Max heard that, and you didn't defend me. You come out with a, 'she shouldn't have called Bailey that word' reasoning? How about 'Bailey's not a prostitute'?" The fire cooled, the anger dropping to a simmer as my voice lowered. "Unless that's how you see this. You pay me to care for Max and expect something on the side."

"I did defend you! I told my mom she had no right to call you that and to mind her own damn business. And Max—" He groaned, and something thumped against the door. Whether that was his head or his fist, I couldn't tell. "I'm sorry I didn't say exactly what you wanted me to say with him, but I wanted to end the discussion immediately. I hated that you'd been called it at all. Even the idea you're one is preposterous, which is why it didn't occur to me to tell Max you aren't. Of course you aren't."

And yet, he didn't deny it when it counted. I sank to the floor, unwilling to open myself up for more disappointment. Unable to be the one to walk away from the door.

"Words hurt, Josh," I said, my eyes locked on the carpet beneath my toes. His carpet…in his house. Where I no longer seemed to fit. "Words definitely hurt, but sometimes not speaking, not sticking up for someone, hurts even worse. I'm done with this conversation for the night. I'll get up with Max if he needs me, but otherwise, I'm off duty. Leave me alone."

"Bailey—don't do this. This isn't about you being on duty. This is about us. I'm sorry, okay?" Another slump, this one lower. Closer. As if he were kneeling right behind me. "I'm sorry my mother said it, I'm sorry Max overheard it, I'm sorry he asked you about it, and I'm sorry I didn't know the exact right thing to say to defuse the situation. I fuck up sometimes. But I would never intentionally hurt you. Ever. I never intended for my actions to come across like I wasn't standing up for you. Like I didn't care. I do. I care about you so much—"

"Just caring isn't always enough." I pushed off the floor and headed for the en suite bath, needing to get away. Wanting to hide. "Good night, Josh."

I closed the bathroom door, blocking him out. Not wanting to hear whatever else he had to say. And then I sank to the floor, and I cried.

———

The morning sun invaded my room way too soon for my liking. My eyes felt like sandpaper and my cheeks burned, but no more tears fell. I was done crying.

It was time to figure out how to move forward and whether Josh was part of that or not.

I wanted him to be.

Hours of wallowing had left me with a clarity that screamed. I didn't want to walk away from Josh and Max. I may not have been ready to forgive him just yet—I had a right to be mad—but this miscommunication wasn't a deal-breaker.

I headed downstairs in my pajamas, unshowered and without makeup. I wanted to make sure Max was okay, and I needed to speak with Josh.

Both my boys were in the kitchen when I got there. Max looked adorably rumpled as he ate a bowl of cereal. And Josh… Scruffy face, bags under his eyes, a paleness to his face that normally wasn't there—he looked as if he hadn't slept a wink. He also didn't look up when I walked in.

"Hey, Maxie." I kissed Max's head. He wasn't as hot as he'd been last night, which meant his fever had broken. "Feeling better?"

"Yeah," he said. "Daddy gave me the orange medicine. He said I had to take it even though I like the pink better."

"I'll make sure to get the pink next time we need it, okay?"

Josh's head popped up, and his worried eyes met mine. "We've got almost a full bottle of the orange."

I shrugged, saying what I could without saying all I needed to. Little ears and all that. "That's fine. I'll make a note on the box so I remember."

"It could be months."

"Then it's months." I ran a finger over his hand as I walked past him. "Maybe if the two of us put our heads together, we'll remember."

I was reaching for a bowl in the top cabinet when Josh came up behind me. He didn't touch, but he was close. So close I could feel his breath on my neck.

"Does that mean you're going to be here in a few months?"

The hope in his voice made me shiver. "I'll be here as long as you want me to be."

He sighed, inching closer, his hand coming to rest next to mine. "Bailey, I'm so—"

"Not now," I whispered, turning to look at him over my shoulder. "I'm still mad, and I don't want to fight in front of Max."

"But later? We'll talk?"

I leaned against him, sighing as his chest met my back. "Definitely. Just let me be mad for a while."

"You can be mad however long you need…" He pressed a quick, stealthy kiss to my forehead, leaving his lips close enough to brush my skin as he whispered, "As long as you don't leave."

I took my bowl to the table and grabbed the cereal box. "So, boys. What's the plan for today other than making sure my little Max here stays on the healthy end of the spectrum?"

"We should probably lie low until he's feeling better," Josh said.

"But, Daddy," Max whined. "I missed family picnic night."

Josh ruffled Max's hair on the way back to his

seat, the doctor in him shining through when his hand flattened against his son's forehead for a quick temperature check.

"I know, buddy." Josh caught my eye as he reclaimed his seat, looking as if he was speaking to me even though I knew his words were meant for Max. "How about a movie day in my room?"

"With all of us, though," Max said.

"If that's okay with Bailey…"

I shrugged, trying not to think about anything else that had happened recently in that room. "Sure. That sounds like fun."

And it did, so long as we avoided any discussion of prostitutes and unspoken words. Which was why I was a bit nervous when, ten minutes later, I walked into Josh's room with my special movie-night blanket.

"What are we watching?" I asked as I took the spot to Max's right. Josh lay on Max's other side, reclined on the bed, his back against the headboard and his legs stretched out and crossed at the ankles. The epitome of calm. Something I wasn't feeling.

"*Mary Poppins*," Max said as he leaned against me. "Those kids get a spoonful of sugar with their medicine."

Josh chuckled and pulled Max a little closer, his arm brushing mine as he did. "Remember when we talked about things in movies not always being real? That's one of those things. Can't have sugar with your medicine, or you'll get a mouthful of cavities and a tummyache."

Josh kept his arm around Max, but his hand was

on my elbow. Holding lightly, almost cautiously. I caught Josh's eyes over Max's head and smiled, letting him know his touch was okay. Welcomed, even. The tension grew between us, turning warmer. More meaningful. This was going to be the longest movie ever.

"Look," Max yelled, sitting up suddenly and pointing to the screen. "They're hiring the nanny. That's how you hired Bailey, right, Daddy?"

"Yep, she blew away the competition." He held my gaze as he said, "As soon as I met her, I knew she was the only one I wanted."

Sometimes, people said one thing that might possibly mean another. Josh did not fall into that group, not that time. I raised my eyebrows, hearing the double meaning just fine. "As soon as you met me? I don't seem to remember it being that easy."

He tried to scowl, though it looked more like a pout. As if he'd just realized how much time we'd wasted. Silly man. "Maybe not, but everything fell into place pretty perfectly."

Max threw his head back, grinning up at me. "Practically perfect in every way, just like Mary Poppins."

There was no fighting back the smile when my Maxie looked at me like that. When he said such cute but significant things. Still, as soon as Max refocused on the movie, I went back to checking out his dad.

"Pretty perfectly, huh?"

"Well, maybe not yet. But soon. I hope."

I wasn't quite ready to say that back, but I couldn't

help the way my smile spread. I hoped for the same. Life with Max and Josh? Being a real family? I couldn't have even dared to wish for such things before.

Though, as we settled in to watch the movie, my thoughts pulled me back to doubt. What would happen once Max started school and I wasn't needed? What would I do? What would Josh want? So many things to think about, to discuss, but there was no way to do that with a five-year-old singing "Supercalifragilisticexpialidocious" between us.

Soon, Josh had said. And he seemed to mean it, if the light touches and sweet smiles he sent my way throughout the movie were any indication. He ran his fingers along my forearm as the old lady implored people to feed the birds; moved down to my palm when the chimney sweeps danced. Every aspect of the movie took on new meaning for me, played out in a way that fed into my hopes and fears of my relationship with Josh. And Max, of course.

When we reached the end, when Mary left the Banks children with their parents and flew off in search of other little ones who needed her help, Max turned to me with a frown on his face.

"You won't leave like Mary Poppins, right, Bee? I still need you."

I shot a panicked look to Josh, completely unsure how to answer. I couldn't just decide to stay. I was technically an employee, and it was Josh's decision in the end.

And still, I couldn't leave my little guy so worried. "I don't want to leave you, Maxie. Who else would call me Bee and make me sing silly songs?" I held Josh's eyes as I said, "I'd be pretty miserable without my boys in my life."

"We'd be miserable without you," Josh said. "Wouldn't we, buddy?"

"The most miserable," Max agreed.

"You love Bailey, huh?"

Max nodded and curled into my side. "Yep, a lot."

"I love her a lot, too." Josh reached for me, his hand slipping around my shoulder as far as he could make it with Max lying between us. "I love her, and I want her to be with us for a long time. As long as she'll have us."

I was trembling hard enough that Josh grabbed my hand where it lay to the side of Max. I weaved my fingers through his, clinging to the hope his words allowed to bloom. "That might be forever, you know."

"Then we'd be pretty lucky."

I bit my lip, grinning around it. "I feel the same way."

Forever with my boys? My family? That sounded like heaven. Which was why, once the movie was over and Josh had put Max down for a nap, I made sure to meet him at his bedroom door.

"Forever, huh? Sounds like quite a commitment."

"Is that what you need to know I'm serious about this? You? Us? A commitment? 'Cause I can go get a ring right now…" Josh reached for me, his hands landing on my hips in the most natural and right move I'd ever experienced. Which was why I let him grab me, allowed him to pull me closer. Consented to being enveloped by him…even as I shook my head.

"I don't need all that. I'd rather you stay right here. With me. Preferably without all this clothing in the way."

He groaned out a laugh, his hands sliding down, cupping my ass in a way that told me more about what he wanted than any words could. "There's not much else I'd rather do. But I need you to know I meant what I said in there. All of it." He pulled away, just enough to grab my hand. My left one. To run his thumb over my ring finger. "I love you, Bailey. And I want you in my life—our lives—forever."

The weight of the past day evaporated in an instant. I wasn't going to be pushed aside or gotten rid of when Max started school. I wasn't a temporary plaything for Josh, either. This was my family, my home, my future…and I wanted to celebrate that.

"I love you, too," I said as I rose onto the balls of my feet and pulled Josh down. I planted my lips on his, demanding in a way I'd never been with him, needy in ways I had. Josh kissed me back just as passionately, at least, until I pushed him away.

"I love you," I said as I pulled my shirt over my head. "But we've only got about two hours before that little boy wakes up and demands every bit of our attention."

"So what are you saying?" Josh smiled and took a step back, pulling me with him, leading us into his bedroom. Well…maybe our bedroom? Shit, too much to think about. At that moment, all that mattered was Josh and me.

"I've always heard make-up sex can be amazing." I

dropped my shorts as I helped him yank his shirt over his head. "How about you show me if that's true?"

He herded me back in slow but determined steps, stalking us toward the bed. "You want me to show you with my mouth or my cock?"

I frowned, purposely pouting my bottom lip. "Why do I have to choose one or the other? Can't I have both?"

epilogue

JOSHUA

"I TELL YOU I'll take you anywhere for our date, and you pick Sin," I said, squeezing Bailey's hand and tugging her closer to me as we walked toward the front door.

She laughed and leaned into my side, hip checking me in the process. "I let you take me to lunch, too, remember? I can't help it if Harper has impeccable timing. She called and said my new toy was in." She pulled me to a stop, then stood on the balls of her feet and nipped at my ear. "Since we've got an empty house, I thought you might want to try it out with me tonight. Was I wrong?" She dropped down so her feet were flat on the ground and stared up at me with a smirk on her face, an eyebrow raised.

"Are you baiting me, baby?" I reached out and palmed her ass, tugging her into my body. Letting her feel exactly what the talk of her with her toys did to me. I took her mouth in a heated kiss, slipping my tongue between her lips when she moaned. Every time she let me kiss her, I was reminded just how lucky I was that she was mine.

When Bailey was breathing hard, her face flushed, the tips of her perky tits rubbing all over my chest and turning my already hard cock into a fucking mountain range in my pants, I pulled back. "Unless you want me to fuck you up against the building, you better get your sweet ass inside and pick up what you need. It's been too long since I've been inside you."

She breathed out a laugh. "It's only been six hours."

I bent down and scraped my teeth along the column of her neck, bringing a hand up between us to brush a thumb over her nipple. "Like I said…"

She shuddered, her breath coming out in a near moan as she relaxed into me. Then with a hand against my chest, she pushed away, shaking her head as if to clear it. "You'd better behave. Church is letting out."

With a quick glance at the red-bricked sanctuary across the street, she tugged me by the hand, leading us to the front door. I held it open for her, following after her as she walked in.

"Nanny Bailey!" Harper called. "You got here fast."

"You called while we were having lunch on Main Street. Besides, I've been waiting for this one for weeks!"

Harper laughed. "Let me grab it for you. Be right back out."

"What kind of fancy bells and whistles does this one have that I can't compete with?" I asked.

"Rotating nubs at the base with a curved tip and a clit stimulator?"

"Pretty sure you competed with that one just fine." She laughed. "This one isn't quite that fancy. It's just supposed to simulate oral." Completely oblivious to my reaction, she headed for the counter.

Narrowing my eyes, I came up behind her, slipping my hand around her waist as she waited at the cash wrap. I tucked a couple fingers into the waistband of her jeans, brushing my fingers along the soft skin of her stomach, then lowered my head until my lips were right at her ear. "Is this your way of telling me I'm not licking your pussy enough? Because by my count, I have you for at least one meal a day. You need my tongue inside you more than that, baby?"

Her stomach clenched against my hand, her breath shuddering out of her as she sank back into me. Resting her head against my chest, she looked up at me, her face flushed, lips parted. Yeah, tonight was going to be fun. I wondered if there was an alcove or something we could sneak away to…

"All right, you two. Save it for home. I like to hear play-by-plays, but I don't need a front row seat to the show."

Bailey jerked away from me with a beaming smile on her face and spun toward Harper, clearly eager to get her new toy. I laughed at her excitement, then pulled out my card when Harper gave the total.

"Hey," Bailey said, a frown marring her lips as she turned to me. "I thought we talked about this. I don't need you to pay my way."

By "talked about this," she meant we had a full-blown fight about it. Bailey hadn't wanted me to continue paying her to be the nanny when Max transitioned into full-day kindergarten. She'd argued that stay-at-home moms didn't get paid to watch their kids, which was essentially what she was doing. Even though Max wasn't biologically hers, she loved him like he was—something I would be eternally grateful for. After my wife passed away, I hadn't thought Max and I would ever find someone to fill the void left. And then we'd found Bailey.

She'd been so adamant about it, I'd conceded, albeit reluctantly. Still, I'd refused her offers to pay for any household bills. Her stay-at-home mom argument had worked against her there, because moms certainly didn't pay rent, either.

The day Max had started school, she'd gotten a part-time job handling the social media accounts for a handful of local businesses. She was well on her way to launching her own public relations firm once she finished school, and the work gave her enough money to cover the expenses she refused to let me pay for, while still being able to care for Max before and after school. So far, it had seemed to work well for all of us.

I leaned down so we were at eye level, her breaths sweeping across my lips. Oh, how easy it would be to close that distance and take her mouth again… "I'd buy you a hundred of these if you promise we'll have as much fun as we did with the last toy you brought home."

"Honey," Harper said to Bailey as she grabbed my credit card. "When a man wants to buy you sex toys, you *let* him. It's not like you're the only one getting pleasure from it…" She raised her eyebrows at Bailey, who laughed in response.

"You have a point."

Once everything was tucked in a tasteful black bag, Harper passed it to Bailey. "You two kids have fun today. Don't do anything I wouldn't do."

"What's that leave, exactly?" Bailey asked. "I can't really see you saying no to much."

"I'll try anything once," Harper said with a wink. "Now I just gotta find someone to try it all with me."

With a laugh and our thanks, we headed toward the front door. I pushed it open ahead of Bailey at the same time it was being pulled open from outside.

"Pastor Noah!" I glanced at him as he stood ramrod straight in his pleated khaki pants, crisp white button-down, and polka-dot bow tie. "I gotta say I wasn't anticipating running into you here."

"Mr. Hutton. Miss Effingham." He nodded politely, but his shoulders were stiff, his mouth set in a hard line. Something had definitely gotten under his skin. "Please excuse me. I need to speak to—"

"Pastor No," Harper called. "You just can't stay away from Sin, can you?"

"Miss Davis, I've asked you repeatedly to call me Noah. Like the rest of the congregation."

"Ah, but I'm not part of your congregation, now am I?"

I glanced at Bailey who was watching the verbal

sparring match with interest. Settling my hand on the small of her back, I leaned down to whisper in her ear, "I thought someone wanted her pussy licked?"

"If these two play their cards right, I won't be the only one trying out a new toy or two." She smiled up at me and reached for my hand. "Let's go home. We've got about eighteen hours before Max comes home from your mom's. I'd like to be naked with you for all of them."

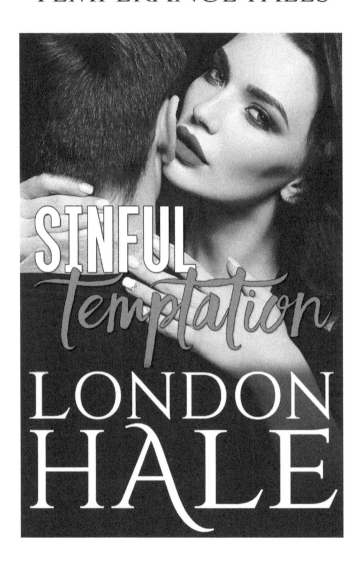

SINFUL
temptation

LONDON
HALE

She's too sinful to resist

I escaped my hometown the second I could, only to be brought back by my late grandmother's will. The Christian bookstore and tea shop she bequeathed to me was the perfect place to open the island's only adult toy store. Being across the street from a church is a bonus. Even better? The new to town, hot as sin pastor I'd love nothing more than to sully. Pastor Noah may be off-limits, but that won't stop me from tempting him.

He could lose it all if he gives in

He could lose it all if he gives in
Sin is my greatest obsession and my congregation's biggest distraction. Harper—the owner of the aptly named adult store—is too forward, too overtly sexual for such a quiet island town, which is why I can't keep my eyes off her. One chance encounter, one moment of surrender, and my fate is sealed. No amount of praying will absolve me of these sins.

about the author

London Hale is the combined pen name of writing besties Ellis Leigh and Brighton Walsh. Between them, they've published more than thirty books in the contemporary romance, paranormal romance, and romantic suspense genres. Ellis is a *USA Today* bestselling author who loves coffee, thinks green Skittles are the best, and prefers to stay in every weekend. Brighton is multi-published with Berkley, St. Martin's Press, and Carina Press. She hates coffee, thinks green Skittles are the work of the devil, and has never heard of a party she didn't want to attend. Don't ask how they became such good friends or work so well together—they still haven't figured it out themselves.

www.londonhale.com

CPSIA information can be obtained
at www.ICGtesting.com
Printed in the USA
LVHW101420180722
723774LV00015B/91

9 781944 336288